Don't Mind Me,
I Came with the House

A novel by

CJ Zahner

Author of:
Friends Who Move Couches
The Suicide Gene
Dream Wide Awake
Project Dream

For information contact Cyndie Zahner
www.cyndiezahner.com

Published 2021
Printed in the United States of America
Print ISBN: 978-1-7332391-2-7
First Printing, 2021
www.cjzahner.com

In memory of Donna Mae Gifford Filutze.
How I wish we could have been fifty years old together.
Miss you every day, Mom.

Chapter One - The wedding

Today, Evy is marrying Bennett. I swipe the mascara wand up my lashes and wonder how many people trust their "until death do us part" person. Especially people I call do-overs—like Evy and me—divorcees who decided "or worse" didn't include cheating, but we are willing to glove up for a second round.

How do you trust an "I do" after you've barely survived a "Not anymore, I don't"?

I'm perched on a barstool in a North Carolina beach bungalow, staring into a mirror set out on a kitchen counter. Worry collects on the big green glob of envy rolling around in my belly. I'm dating Bennett's twin brother, Blake, who's never once brought up the "m" word.

I hope this relationship doesn't spontaneously combust like my twenty-year marriage did.

I trust Blake. I do. There's just this itty-bitty worry that I'm too common for him, that his out-of-town trips hide some fantastic life I can't compete with.

Plus, there's the annoying matter of his popularity. People knock me down to get to him. As if I'm invisible. A portrait on the wall that no one notices.

Until it's crooked.

I pitch my mascara into my makeup bag and gaze around the room for a diversion to my wedding thoughts—correction—my no-wedding thoughts. I spot the chocolate-cream-stuffed donuts encased in cellophane, sitting ten feet from me. Eating one will upset my stomach but, worse, Evy will notice one's missing and have a conniption.

Everett, Evy, is a good friend. A trusted confidant. But he's no Anderson Cooper. Just a middle-aged father of two. College professor. Philosopher, sort of. A gay commoner in modern-day society. A person never tempted to keep his opinion to himself. He is…

He's impossible. He'll kill me if I eat one.

"Mom, can you help me—" My daughter, Delanie, bursts into the room like a flaming comet, while my thoughts of Evy and fitting into the dress I'm wearing to his beach wedding tango toward the donuts. Her fiery voice jolts me back to the tasks at hand: finishing my makeup, polishing Evy's rings.

She stops and blinks hard. "What happened to your face?"

Her arms overflow with little bouquets, their white chiffon streamers dangling in disarray. Normally, she ignores me, so her attention alarms me. I glance back to the mirror and see black everywhere. "Oh, great."

"Don't move." She plops the bouquets on the counter, plucks a makeup wipe out of a container, and her thin fingers grip my chin like a vice.

"Ouch," I whimper.

"Sit still."

She scrapes my cheeks like she's stripping varnish off an antique. When she's finished, her gaze darts back and forth across my face. "You'll have to reapply your base."

She releases her grasp, and I cradle my chin in my hand. "That hurt."

She pats her hands with a paper towel then points a finger at me. "Do not ruin this for Evy."

Delanie is my oldest child. She's twenty-one years old going on sixty and suffers from role reversal. She thinks she's my mother.

"I won't," I swear.

"Promise?" She plants her hands on her hips.

"I do. I promise." I'm a mother afraid of her own. First-born children, in particular, scare me.

"Do you have the rings?"

My stomach flexes like a fist.

"I do. Right here. See?" I flick the little box open and set it on the counter.

She sighs. I think she's disappointed I haven't lost Evy's treasured bands.

"I'm polishing them." I grab the silver cleaner and wave it in the air.

"Don't mess it up," she says, then screams her sister's name with the power of Ursula. "Gianna. Can you help me hang the flowers on the chairs? Mom's not ready."

Evy's delegated the part of the wedding planner to me for this momentous occasion, which is monumental since he's a maniac when it comes to details. His reasoning for my appointment is threefold. First, I'm a dynamite designer with an eye for color schemes. Second, I crave perfection. (I fall a tad short here.) And third, my family gives more attention to gnats in our basement than to me. Evy believes planning his wedding will reveal my hidden beauty and talent to my children—not to mention Blake. In other words, Evy's a good friend and he's doing this for me.

I'm not proud. I welcome his pity job.

To perfect every minor detail of the wedding and increase my family's ability to see my finer qualities, I've petitioned all three of my children to help co-plan the event. (Keep your friends close. Your enemies, closer.)

We are staying at an upscale resort on the coast, which I located and Evy paid for. He rented ten suites for family and friends. Blake, the best man, has entrusted me with the rings.

Big mistake. Blake's faith in me never ceases to amaze me. My ex-husband wouldn't trust me with a nickel at a dime store.

Mark, my first, was a nightmare. Blake, hopefully my second, is a dream. Now every morning when the sun slips through my window and I open my eyes, I remember my old life is gone, and I smile in sheer ecstasy. No more Marks. Only Blakes.

When he doesn't have a tournament—Blake's one flaw is golf—and my older kids are away at college and my youngest is at a sleepover, I wake up on weekend mornings beside him, feeling like I've hit the relationship lottery. The whole you-marry-once Catholic guilt hits me every Sunday, but not enough for me to hide my tail between my legs and crawl back to Mark. I like Blake too much.

Plus, other people enjoy his company. Much more than they did Mark's.

Blake is endearing. And he's a golf pro, which automatically boosts any guy who's rated a seven out of ten to a nine. Blake's a nine to start, elevating him to the sought-after ten-plus category.

"When you're done—" Delanie commands me away from my wandering thoughts. She shouts over one shoulder as she scurries out the door. "Come help Gianna and me."

I hear five or six loud thumps on the staircase, and Gianna bounds into the room like an antelope. She's grown as tall as her sister, her long, lean body pretty in pink, a wide smile gracing her blue eyes, pug nose, and perfect cheekbones. Despite the bad first marriage, I wouldn't change a day. Mark and I produced three great kids.

"What happened to your cheeks?" Her forehead wrinkles.

"Why?" I gaze into the mirror.

"They're red."

"They are, aren't they?" I apply a base to cover the vandalism Delanie's hands have strewn about my face, then sit back and inspect myself. "I'll touch it up before the ceremony," I say, then gaze at my daughter.

She pinches the sides of her dress. "How do I look?"

My children's growth spurts, both physical and mental, spark teary-eyedness in me. Gianna, my baby, grew up overnight during the divorce. Today, Delanie has dusted her face with makeup. A hint of sugary perfume wafts toward me as she sways back and forth. But for her wildly happy eyes, someone might mistake her for a sixteen-year-old. At fourteen, that thrashing attitude toward her mother hasn't yet settled in. She still likes me.

Occasionally.

"You look beautiful." I hug her.

"Let go of me. You'll wrinkle my dress."

"It's skintight. You'd have to iron a wrinkle on."

Her expression turns. "Can't you, for once, say something nice? You always have to ruin everything."

There you go. The little-girl moment dashed. Her shoulders stiffen and her teeth clench.

With daughters, bursts of independence surface in the single-digit years. By ten, they've realized their friends stack blocks better than their mother. By twelve, you annoy them. Fourteen, you embarrass them. Sixteen, you appall them, and at eighteen you can't grab their attention with a foghorn. They deflect your voice, advice, instruction, guidance. Everything you offer them comes sailing back faster than a boomerang whirled by a weightlifter—except money. I've sunk half of my 401k into these girls.

Then they advance to their twenties, and suddenly, you're the child and they're the mother.

Life was easier when they were two, and I told them to do this, don't do that, do everything exactly the way Mommy tells you. And they did. Joyfully. Their eyes twinkled and their faces lit up when I walked into a room. Now they run when they see me. Have the audacity to advise me. Point out how I might improve my life as if wisdom is a regressive trait we are born with and lose over time.

I miss the old days when they gazed at me adoringly.

"You're so negative," she hollers, and the knot in my stomach tightens. "Just once, can't you be nice?"

Her inappropriate dress shimmies a half-inch down the front of her, but I say nothing because "your bandage bodycon fits you like skin on a snake," would send her venom spewing. Silently, I watch her long hourglass shape march away. Inwardly,

I scold myself for getting caught up in a dress-buying moment with my girls.

Evy has played an important role in my children's lives since they were little. We celebrated when he found Bennett. Where normally we don't agree on much, the girls and I concurred that Bennett was the best thing to happen to Evy. Tittering with happiness and wanting to make him proud of us, his friend family, we slipped into a dress shop, and I became enamored with the moment, conceded to Gianna's begging, and purchased the dress that now flaunts my fourteen-year-old's breasts like an eighteen-year-old's.

"You look wonderful." I wave the tip of an olive branch toward her.

She slams the screen door on its leaves. "Whatever."

When I was pregnant with Gianna, my third child, I begged God for a girl. I wanted Delanie to have someone she could walk hand in hand with through life, too. I didn't count on them ganging up and sending me to an early grave.

Sometimes God steps in to answer our prayers at the most inopportune times.

I dance in frivolous thought for several minutes until, tiredly, I waddle off the daughter topic and back to the wedding, where a minor detail slaps me.

I run to the door and holler to Gianna and Delanie. "I forgot. The slipcovers are in those boxes on the altar. Can you start covering chairs until I get there?"

"You've got to be kidding. You tell us now? I've fixed flowers on three rows." Delanie steps away so I can see her picture-perfect work.

"I'm sorry." I bite my lip with one front tooth. "Could you redo them? The covers are dressy, perfect for an outdoor wedding."

"You are so hung up on perfect."

I am. I admit it. Don't we yearn for what we lack?

"I want this day to be perfect. For Evy. You know how he is." I deflect blame with the best of the cowards.

"Nothing is perfect, Mom. Not you, me, this wedding, the stupid chairs. And who cares?" Delanie huffs and puffs and I think she might blow the entire white plastic makeshift altar down as she stomps toward the box of slipcovers.

"I care." I step outside.

"Of course, you do. You want to impress everyone that you're this wonderful person. You want to be—" She shakes her head primly. "Noticed." Then she spews, "But the truth of the matter is Evy couldn't care less if his wedding is perfect."

"You're wrong. Evy does care."

"No, he doesn't." Despite the distance between us, I see the frustration in her eyes. "Evy will love us even if this ceremony is a complete disaster. You're the person who doesn't understand life."

I'm uncertain how to respond. There's probably some truth buried in her budding philosophical moment, but all I can think right now is she doesn't know Evy.

"Go in the house and stay out of the way." She opens the box, grabs two chair covers, and trudges toward the first row.

I tramp inside, determined not to allow her to ruin my mood. I tidy up the kitchen then retrieve the prepared fruit platters and set them out beside the donuts and Danish for the brunch after the ceremony. I fill the crystal punchbowl Evy's inherited from his grandmother with orange juice and champagne, dump pineapple-shaped ice cubes in the middle, and stir.

I resume my seat at the counter, reach for the rings, and take my frustration with my girls out on the wedding bands, polishing the heirlooms to perfection. As I finish, I see Blake's reflection as he enters the suite behind me.

"Hello, gorgeous." He strides toward me, his tailored black suit embellishing his squared shoulders, thin waist, lean legs. He sneaks a kiss on the nape of my neck. "Rumor has it you have this suite to yourself tonight. Your kids are staying with mine in the room by the pool, right?"

"They are. They don't want me ruining their good time. How'd you convince Delanie to watch your girls tonight?" My kids will do anything for Blake. "She's always so agreeable for you."

"I pay her exorbitantly." He sets his hands on my shoulders and squeezes. I shiver. "Nice job on the rings, by the way."

"Thanks. I think Delanie secretly hoped I'd rinse them down the drain."

Blake sneaks a hand onto the counter and drags the paper towel and rings away from the sink. "No sense tempting you."

"Ye of little faith. They're drying. I'll have them out to you in a minute." I stand and slip my arms around his waist.

"You look beautiful." His eyes wander over me.

"Thank you." I move my eyebrows up and down. "You don't look half bad yourself."

"Why are you getting ready here?"

"Oh." I release my grip and gather my makeup into its bag. "The girls were hogging the bathrooms."

He turns me around, places a hand on the small of my back, and exhales warm breath beneath my ear. "How much time do we have before the service?"

Chills rush down my neck and across my shoulders. "Not that much time."

He stands back, laughing. "Okay, Nikki Grey, I'll see you—"

"Stone," I exclaim. "I'm no longer drab and boring Nikki Grey. Remember? I'm drab and boring Nikki Stone."

I took my maiden name back after my divorce. Long story short: my ex had a child with another woman while we were married, and I refuse to share a last name with the two of them.

"I'm sorry. I mean Nikki Stone." Blake draws me toward him again as if he can't keep his hands off me. His rich, intoxicating cologne makes me dizzy. "Maybe someday we'll do something about that drab and boring last name."

He kisses me but I don't feel a thing. I'm afraid my mind is playing tricks on me. What did he say? Did he mean…my name…might be his someday? Anderson? As in Mrs. Blake Anderson?

When he leaves, I stand dazed like a teenage girl after the captain of the football team has winked at her. This is a first.

Suddenly the temperature of the room skyrockets, and I begin perspiring profusely. I wiggle inside my clothes. My underwear and dress cling to my body. The hair falling on my neck frizzes. My makeup slides down my cheeks. I fan my face but can't stop sweating. I'm a perfect menopausal mess. I grab for a paper towel on the counter and pat myself dry at the exact moment I hear metal clinking.

I stop breathing. My gaze falls to the sink. I'm paralyzed as I watch two rings roll round and round until the big, ugly hole in the middle sucks them into the underworld.

"No, no, no, no," I cry.

The drain. I jinxed myself.

I reach my hand down under and a mangle of food tangles with sharp metal prongs. I gag, recoil my food-stained fingers, lean over the sink, and gaze into the depths of hell.

Above me, a light fixture dangles from the ceiling. I reach and flip its switch, but instead of casting light onto the hellhole, I hear grinding and whirring and scraping and clunking, a rhythmic melody of doom.

I pirouette into a hyperventilating attack so quickly that the dry grinding sounds nearly send me to the floor. I regain my composure and flick the garbage disposal switch off. I take a deep breath—I don't know why I'm holding my breath—and force my hand into the muck and grime of the sinkhole.

"Don't faint," I tell myself.

I was born with temporal lobe epilepsy, and if I pass out, I will lose my driver's license for six months or until I haven't had a seizure for six months. Two years ago, I had my first devastating episode—a grand mal—after foolishly smoking marijuana with friends. Up until that fateful day, I'd only had partial seizures; brief annoying moments where I stared subconsciously.

"Don't seize!" I command as I slop a mucky mess into the sink, gagging. Two hints of silver glimmer through a stringy glob of greenish-black goop. I grab them with my free hand and use an elbow to turn the water on only to realize the faucet is on the spray setting. Water drenches me just as the processional music begins outside.

Wonderful.

With one eye open, I turn the water to stream and wash the gunk off Evy's rings. I set them on the side and rinse the grime from my arms, but my dress, hair, and makeup are ruined beyond quick repair.

I grab the edge of the counter and breathe. Blackness tries to weasel its way into my vision, but I stand my ground. I'm not going down. Slowly, my head clears. I rinse the putrid muck down the sink and examine the rings. Evy's is pecked like a dartboard and Bennett's is pear-shaped, the engraved words that Evy's so carefully chosen for him laugh up at me: Our love is a circle of perfection.

Not anymore, it's not.

My stomach has been so upset in the past few weeks that now I have to do everything I can not to throw up on the floor. I slip the rings into the box and hurry outside. I'm soaked, hair dripping, makeup stinging my eyes, but what can I do? The ceremony has begun, and I'm clutching the ring box.

Blake is standing at the altar beside Bennett and when he gazes my way, he does a double-take and goes slack-jawed as if he's glimpsed Medusa. Then, slowly, his shock melts, and his lips part into that forever smirk I usually love on him but don't appreciate today. Seven rows of people separate us, and I'm tempted to heave the ring box over their heads and run.

Instead, I make my way down the side closest to him, ignoring the snickers. Bennett glances over his shoulder to see what the tittering is about and, although he and Blake aren't identical twins, a smirk lifts his lips and his expression mirrors the same easily-amused mien of his brother's.

On the other side of the altar, Evy gives me a once over as if I'm a zombie rising from the marshlands.

By the time I hand off the rings, Blake and Bennett, shoulders shaking, can't make eye contact with me. I hear my son laughing and my girls sighing, so when I turn, I steer away from the empty seat in the front row beside them and march down the aisle, searching for my friend Jody. I spot her motioning toward the chair beside her. I step over two people and slouch into the seat, glad that at least my disheveled appearance has kept Blake from spotting the mangled rings.

The giggles simmer then cease. Ten minutes later Blake opens the ring box. Evy looks me straight in the eye and says, "Naggy, darling." Naggy is the nickname he uses for me when he's angry or bothered. "I'm going to string you up by your ankles and pull every hair off your head, one by one. Then I'll shred your closet."

My stomach gurgles, I belch, and then I projectile vomit on the three people sitting in front of me.

Perfect.

Chapter - Two The apology

If Evy is correct and reincarnation exists, I'm coming back as a mom who is appreciated more and thinks less.

More than a week has passed since Evy's wedding, and Delanie and Gianna still aren't speaking to me. Their constant annoyance with me spins on a wheel in my head. Like a worry machine in a twenty-four-hour shop. Thoughts keep coming, cutting, spiraling.

Delanie stomps down the stairs this morning in a bad mood. She was out late last night and can't hide her puffy eyes, even with hydrating cream, which I know she's used since a smidge of it is caked on the side of one eye. I don't dare tell her. Fire will shoot out of her nostrils.

"Good morning," I say, instead.

She ignores me and heads straight for the coffee, grabbing a mug from the cupboard then realizing there are no k-cups in the holder. She slams the cup on the counter and sighs disgustedly.

"There are some in the pantry," I inform her.

She groans, my voice as insignificant as the hum of the refrigerator. "This place is a mess," she mumbles to herself.

It's a Saturday morning in June. My two college kids are home for the summer, and my high school student and her two friends are upstairs, still sleeping after their loud all-nighter. Bowls and glasses crowd my sink. Pizza boxes hide my kitchen table. Pop cans flood the recycling bin.

Delanie passes on the coffee and tramps out of the kitchen without acknowledging my presence in the slightest.

"You left your keys on the sofa. I dropped them in your purse," I holler.

No response.

The door slams shut, and my worry-milling brain returns to its clinking and clanging as it roils. I gather up the kitchen garbage along with the annoying swarf my mind spews. The cutting shards of rebuttals stockpile in my brain as I carry on, perpetually grinding. I'm in jeopardy of catching fire. Self-combusting.

"You left the garage door open last night." The sound of my son's deep voice jolts me. Hux, my rambunctious, carefree middle child, who spends half of his life eating and the other half teasing his sisters, has appeared out of nowhere.

"I closed it for you. You're welcome," he adds.

While uttering thank you is something my children find unnecessary, they expect me to thank them profusely if they pick their own toenail clippings off the floor.

"Thanks." I chew on my lip, swallow those rebuttals.

"Is Evy home? Can you ask him if I can borrow his kayaks?"

There's no "hi, Mom," "good morning," "how are you feeling?" He needs a favor, and it's as if I've been standing in the kitchen all night waiting to provide one.

"Yes, he's home, but you'll have to ask him yourself."

"Why can't you ask him?"

"Here's a newsflash: I don't exist to serve you, Hux."

"You're a mother. You're supposed to do stuff for your kids."

"I have a life, I'll have you know." There's only so much one mother can take.

"Yeah, okay, mopping floors and scrubbing sinks."

"There is more to my life than frivolous chores."

"Like what?"

Something erupts inside me. Like water dropping into a pan of hot oil. Mentos, into a can of Diet Coke. "Like I'm a living, breathing person. I have wants and needs. Desires."

"Desires?"

"Yeah, desires. Goals. I'm tired of people traipsing by me like I don't exist. I'd like people to respond when I ask a question. Notice me when I walk into a room."

"So, what? You want to be an internet sensation or something?"

"Yeah, maybe I do. Maybe I want to be a sensation, a star for a change."

"Moms are behind-the-scene stars."

While this might be a skewed compliment, my temperature is rising and I can't stop the foamy Coke from brimming. I'm not sure why I'm so emotional. I have to choke back tears. "Behind-the-scenes people are underappreciated. I'm working my fingers raw and none of you care. I don't want to get to the end of my life and realize I haven't accomplished a single thing. That I'm nobody."

"Mom, don't get overdramatic. It's not the end that matters. It's the journey."

Wait, what?

"You worry too much," he says. "Why don't you chill? Sit back, relax. Smell the roses. Enjoy the ride."

Where'd my son go? He's never had an existential moment in his life.

My tear ducts dry. I'm shocked into somberness.

"Is this because you puked at the wedding? You're not still worried Evy's mad, are you? About the rings?"

He's caught me off guard. I raise my chin and respond honestly, "Yes, I am."

"Mom, Evy isn't mad. Bennett used pliers and straightened them out."

In the past week, I tried not to feel guilty over ruining Evy's rings and throwing up on his aunt and cousins, but Evy and Bennett were due home from their honeymoon last night, so I'm mildly anxious.

"The wedding was perfect," Hux continues. "The lamb was to die for. Did you taste it?"

While I annoy my daughters relentlessly, my son couldn't care less about what I say or do. Nothing much bothers him. His current goal in life is scoring free pizza and wings at local restaurants, which he usually accomplishes in a back room with a deck of cards. He's a poker shark. Or a whale. Whichever means good.

"It only seemed perfect for you because you didn't spend two hours scrubbing the carpet." I cross my arms. "All that lamb and you needed pizza at midnight?"

"We were hungry."

"You took the beer from the bar, too, didn't you? There was none left when we cleaned up. I hope you didn't let your little sister or Blake's girls drink."

"No, I didn't."

"You didn't take the beer or you didn't let them drink?"

"Both."

"You're not of legal age, Hux."

"C'mon, Mom, it was Evy's wedding. I had a few cans at the pool. I didn't take any to our suite. I kept it away from the girls."

"I suppose you want a thank you for that."

"A thanks would be nice." He smiles. His eyes twinkle.

"I would have thanked you to clean the pizza out of the carpet."

"Sorry about that, Mom." He steps toward me, plants a kiss on my cheek, and my blood, minutes ago rushing through my veins, slows to a crawl.

He could schmooze the last dollar out of a poor man's pocket. He's been in trouble twice as much as both girls combined but talks his way out of jams with the bat of his long lashes over his baby blues.

"Don't you have someplace to be?" I try to disguise my dissipating anger. I should be punishing him for drinking.

"Work," he replies.

"You're working today?" My voice escalates once again. I think the girls pay him to raise my blood pressure. "Then you're late."

He opens a cabinet and grabs a box of cereal and a bowl. "I had to wake Gianna and her friends. They hate it if I don't say goodbye before I leave. Mind if I take the milk?"

Both of Gianna's friends who spent the night have crushes on Hux. Gianna herself adores him. On the other hand, he disgusts Delanie. He's dated two of her friends. Ex-friends, that is. He broke their hearts.

"Yes, I mind. Gianna and her friends won't have any."

"Girls don't drink milk."

"Get back here with that."

I shake my head then swear at myself when I realize I'm smiling. Hux's dewy words always soften my anger. Opposingly, when my girls walk into a room, my stomach twists, logic nose dives, and my mouth gushes like a fireplug. With sons, it's different. Your emotions bounce back and forth between rage and love like a tennis ball over a net.

"You drove the car into a stop sign?" *Whack.*

"He mowed the lawn." *Tap.*

"You broke the blender?" *Wallop.*

"He ran to the store for me." *Rap.*

"You have to appear before the District Justice?" *Game over.*

Mothers melt around sons, and daughters hate them for it. My girls insist Hux is my favorite child, but he's not. He causes me way more grief. And he can't take care of himself. Can any son? I'll never rush marriage on either of my girls, but I'll be glad for the day when Hux is some other woman's responsibility.

He grabs a spoon and heads out the door.

"Make sure you bring that back. My silverware is disappearing."

"Gotcha." He stuffs it into his pocket, and the screen door slams behind him. There's a zero-percent chance he'll return that spoon.

"Call, Evy. He's not mad," he yells. "And remember. It's all about the journey. Chill out."

Instead of heeding his advice, the mention of Evy restarts my temporarily stalled worry wheel. I do consider his point, however. Is Evy still mad?

A simple apology doesn't seem fitting for ruining the rings, so I cook a lasagna-and-meatball peace platter. I spend half the day simmering ground beef, sautéing peppers and onions, and perfecting my red sauce. When I drop it off, Evy and Bennett gush with happiness in seeing me, and I wonder if they've lost their memory.

Vacationing for ten days has dampened Evy's ire—vacationing and Bennett. I'm beginning to wonder if Blake and Bennett Anderson have a single flaw between them. Intelligent, compassionate, handsome, and each athletic in his own way, the two might not be identical twins, but they are identically endearing. Neither possesses an ounce of anger. Like Hux, smirks are plastered on their faces throughout much of life.

I mention this to Evy when Bennett excuses himself for a work call.

"You're right," Evy agrees. "They're blessed with a contentment that others aren't born with."

For a moment I wonder if this is a guy thing. Then I remember Mark's flaring temper and change my mind. "Do you think they're happy because of genes or the way they were brought up?"

Evy shoots me a reflective stare. "I know where that question is going."

"What?"

Bennett isn't gone a minute, and Evy's tone has changed. He sits, scrutinizing me. I can't read his blank stare. Then he reaches across the couch and shocks me by placing his palm over the back of my hand.

"You're a good mother. You love your children unconditionally. They'll turn out fine. My girls will live through my mistakes, and your kids will survive yours."

"But will I survive the guilt over my mistakes?"

"You will." Evy scoots over on the couch, slings an arm around my shoulder, and I lean my head on him. "You are harder on yourself than anyone I know."

The planets must be aligned in some existential orbit today. First Hux offers inspirational advice, now Evy.

"I feel I've failed my family with the whole botched marriage thing."

He leans his chin on the top of my head. "Not so hard you can't forget how bad it was. If it makes you feel better, concentrate on the fact that Mark cheated. Multiple times. And had a child with another woman."

"Are you trying to make me feel better or worse?"

"Better. If he hadn't done those deplorable things, I think you'd still be miserably married to him."

"True." I'd been so engrossed in myself and my three kids during my marriage, I hadn't recognized I was miserable. "But I have that whole Catholic guilt thing going on."

"Well, stick with me, kid. I'll help you relieve yourself of that heavy baggage. I changed your mind on gay people, didn't I?"

I lift my head off his shoulder and smile, a memory lighting the moment. "You did. You completely dashed my gays-go-to-hell upbringing."

"I'll take that as a compliment."

My mother was an ardent Catholic. My father skipped masses but exemplified Christian giving. I was forced to suffer through sixteen years of Catholic education—attending a religious college exponentially magnifies your guilt. Lay teachers and clergy drilled marriage-is-between-a-man-and-a-woman into me. I had been in jeopardy of growing into a Janice Everglade. (The short version of a long story is Janice Everglade is a judgmental bigot.)

Then Evy came along. Evy with the whipping tongue and heart of pure syrup and sugar. What few people know is he donates a portion of his salary to inner-city high school students who want to go to college. He cared for his sick mother until the day she died. Takes his girls to volunteer at a soup kitchen twice a month and has inspired ferocious independence in them though they are only thirteen years old. Luck fell on Leah and Penny when Evy adopted them.

"When Christ came into the world, he bludgeoned lots of beliefs with his number one commandment: Love one another," he adds.

"When did you get all religious on me?"

He recoils his arm. Stretches it along the couch. "I teach a theology class, remember?"

"Val said you teach paint-by-numbers."

Val is Evy's best friend. Jody is mine. Jody moved to Seattle over a year ago, shortly before Mark and I split up. Evy and Val walked me through many a lonely night without her.

"Pottery, my God. You couldn't grasp an academic hand if you were slipping off a yacht in the middle of an ocean."

"Why would I be in a yacht in the middle of an ocean?"

For some reason, I always make light of Evy's serious side. He's so smart I can't banter with him over life's lessons. Stand him beside me on a track, and I'll beat his skinny butt every time. But battle against him in the world-knowledge arena? I'm like a God-fearing Christian fighting a lion.

Evy sees right through me. "You're right, darling, no one with any class would ever invite you on a yacht."

He moves away from me on the couch. I smile and scoot toward him. He slides further away. I inch next to him, thigh-to-thigh.

"You love me," I say.

"You and your one-hundred-and-one IQ," he chides right as Bennett meanders back into the room.

Bennett shakes his head and counters, saying I'm the smartest woman he knows, which isn't that big of a compliment because he hardly knows any women. Yet, the temperature of the room rises to a lovely warmth.

How could anyone suggest these two men were anything less than pure love?

"So, I have to ask." Evy usually gets annoyed when Bennett takes my side. He'll ruffle my feathers now. "When do you think that man of yours will pop the question?"

Bam. A vulnerability slap.

"You had to ruin the moment, didn't you? You warm me up with your Jesus talk then smack me like I'm a sun-basking fly on a beach towel."

"I'm simply preparing you. He will and you better be ready. No tumbling over that long, loose tongue of yours."

"You don't know that he will. He still sees his ex twice a month. I'm just trying to keep my spot on the love seat. Sit a safe distance away so he doesn't see born-loser me."

"That's impossible. Have you forgotten the wedding?" Evy holds a hand to the side of his face and hollers. "He knows you're a disaster."

His hand drops. "I must have been crazy asking you to help plan my wedding."

Bennett steps toward me. "Blake only sees his ex when he drops off the girls. Trust me. That door has closed. My brother drags his feet but only because he's shy; he'll ask."

"Maybe," I say, remembering Blake's comment about changing my last name. "But I need to keep my better side front and center."

"Better? You only have two sides, mis and hap."

"C'mon, Evy. She did a fabulous job on our wedding. It was perfect." Bennett sets a hand on my shoulder, leans, and kisses the top of my head. "Tell her."

"It was nice." This kills Evy to admit.

"Well, just think. If you guys are right and Blake does ask me to marry him?" I pat Evy's knee and stand. "We'll be related."

A horrific realization washes over him.

"We'll spend every holiday together," I add.

Bennett leaves the room laughing, and Evy lectures me to the front door, something about respecting family rules of conduct. I politely ignore him and exit, snickering.

On the ride home and for the remainder of the day, however, I think over what they've said about Blake asking me to marry him. I should be happy. I want to be happy, but I've got this entire throwing-up issue going on that has risen out of nowhere.

I caution myself. I have a bad tendency to view happiness as the calm before the storm—a balminess in the air. It's terrible the way I check life's forecast as if I'm unworthy of sunshine.

I force myself to concentrate on the positive that evening. I take my golden retriever, Furgy, for a long, relaxing walk, and we enjoy the peacefulness of my neighborhood. Afterward, we settle in the family room to watch a frivolous TV show. I sip wine and rub Furgy's back with my toes.

But then I head to the bathroom during a commercial and, OMG, I'm dying.

I haven't had a period in over a year. I'm menopausal. Two doctors confirmed this. Now I'm spotting, which can only mean one thing.

I can't say the word. I can't think it. Surely, the big C has turned Nikki Stone's weather vane. It's a gloomy, forbidden forecast: rain flogged with doom.

Ridiculous thoughts whirl me into a spin. I run to my bedroom and lunge onto the bed dramatically, for effect. I'm not sure whom I think is watching. God? Am I trying to squeeze pity from Him?

Furgy jumps up beside me. I nuzzle my face into her fur and cry myself to sleep, hating Nikki Stone because if she hasn't grown up by forty-seven, she's never going to grow up.

Chapter Three - The gynecologist

I'm sitting underneath a sheet of paper, stark naked, wondering what type of human being wants to be a gynecologist. Not an obstetrician, you can understand that profession. A new life slipping into your hands could make anyone forget the sordid details. But what went through a gynecologist's head on high-school career days? "I'd love to spend my life looking up vaginas?" Or "Wouldn't it be fun to yank a uterus out?"

These people are sick.

I sit on the uncomfortably hard table, pretending I'm not embarrassed. Faces on magazines smile at me from a rack on the wall. I could grab one and read, try to forget someone is about to knead my breasts and poke my cervix, but if I step down and reach for one at the exact moment the doctor opens the door, my paper gown might waft forward and expose my forty-seven-year-old butt.

Not pretty.

So I sit and glance around the room. Stare at the colorful sketches of female parts I don't want to think about, instruments I don't want anything to do with, and a bottle of cream that I fantasize about. I'd like to squeeze every bit of it onto the walls. Blot out everything in the room I don't want to see.

A lubricant to make your exam easier.

The ridiculous thought of covering the place with ointment spreads through my mind like a venereal disease at spring break. Imagine the surprise on Doctor Yank-a-uterus's face if she entered and her elaborate fallopian-tube painting was all creamed up. I snort out a laugh.

For a moment, I forget where I am and relax. Then I shift to a more comfortable position on the table and one knee pokes out from underneath my paper skirt.

I examine my kneecap. Several half-inch hairs point up at me.

Drat.

How'd I miss those? I raise my leg. Longer hairs stick out the back.

My mind dances on to my shaving inabilities. This must be some deep-seated human survival technique. I don't want to think about my exam or worse, a formidable C diagnosis, so I amuse myself with the hair on my knees. Allow my thoughts to tango toward trivialities. I imagine how great life would be if I invented something that shaved a leg perfectly, knees, front and back. I'd secure a patent for the flawless instrument. Become rich. Like the Post-it guy. He made a bundle.

I sigh. I'm waiting for the most uncomfortable examination in the world, fretting about whether I have the big C, and suddenly coarse leg hairs and Post-its matter. I've lost all sensibility.

I lean down and take one last look. Trivial or not, I spent last night shaving every inch of my legs—more than I do for Blake—so how could these hairs of shame be waving up at me?

"Good morning, Mrs. Grey." I nearly pee myself when the doctor surprises me.

"Stone," I say, a tad too loudly. "I've taken my maiden name back."

"Sorry, I'll note that." She taps on her iPad. "So how have you been feeling? Any menopausal symptoms?"

"A few," I say because yelling, "Yes, I sweat profusely. Can't you see my paper robe disintegrating?" might send her into a mood, and Lord knows I want a happy examiner.

She stammers on about this and that. I have to tell her about Mark. Then Blake. Yes, sex is fine. No, I'm not experiencing any pain. What? Oh, yeah, kids are great. Job is fine. Why is she chatting like we're on a coffee date? I want to scream for her to save the small talk for later. Hasn't she ever had an exam herself? Get it over already.

She chatters on about menopause and periods and how spotting is unusual and should be checked out but, blah, blah, blah, I shouldn't worry yet. Finally, she walks to the sink, washes her hands, and tells me to scoot down and put my feet in the stirrups.

I shiver.

Supposedly, the most unpopular word in the English language is moist. I disagree. I vote for stirrups. It shoots electricity through me every time. I lie back, smoldering, pondering the ugliness of what's about to happen beneath my paper sheet. I practice my breathing while Doctor Yank picks and prods like she's at a campfire trying to restart the flames. Right when she is deep into the exam, I hear a knock, and a nurse jars the door open.

"Oh, I'm sorry doctor," she says.

Seriously? I cover my face with both hands in case a husband walks by and recognizes me later in the waiting room.

Isn't that the old lady with the ugly vagina?

"No problem, Aimee, I'm almost done here." She keeps prodding.

"I have the results of Mrs. Grey's tests."

"Stone," I lift my head and yell. A flash of a face passing in the hall behind the nurse startles me. I make eye contact with the person. Are they selling tickets to my exam? I raise my voice. "It's Ms. Stone. Ms. Nikki Stone."

The nurse's neck snaps back, her eyes widen, and the doctor stops prodding. We stare at each other for an uncomfortable few seconds. Of course, can there be a comfortable moment when your legs are spread from wall to wall?

"Thanks, set them on the desk."

After the nurse leaves, I apologize, the doctor is gracious, and, mercifully, the exam ends.

Now the wait is on.

"How long before I know if this is some type of cervical or uterine cancer?" I ask.

"Mrs. Gr—I'm sorry." Fright spreads across her face. She backs up as if I might unloose a foot and lodge it in her mouth. "Ms. Stone, I mean Ms. Stone. I'm fairly certain I know what the problem is. Let me take a look at your results."

Oh, no.

"You can sit up," she says, but I can't. The tone of her voice tells me what her words don't. It's bad news. Worse than expected.

This is the story of my life. Every time a speck of happiness falls my way, a mound of troubles follows. I place a wrist on my forehead and prepare myself for what's to come. I should have known dating the best guy in the world would have drawbacks. Now I'm sick. My love life is perfect so my health is bad. "Oh, my God, I have ovarian cancer, don't I?"

"Ms. Stone, please." She pats the side of the table. "Sit up and we'll talk."

We'll talk?

"Oh, my God." I begin crying. "I shouldn't have come alone. You don't know me. I have temporal lobe epilepsy. I'm not supposed to stress out."

"Ms. Stone—"

"If I have a seizure, I'll lose my driver's license. How will I get to my chemotherapy? I have a daughter in high school. How am I going to tell her? And a boyfriend. He's a wonderful guy. Will I lose my hair? This is the worst thing in the world."

"Ms. Stone," the doctor hollers above my wailing. "You don't have cancer."

I barely hear her through my crying and snorting. "What?"

"You don't have cancer."

"I don't?" I wipe my face and sit up.

"No, you don't."

"Then what's wrong with me? Why am I spotting? My mother's friend, Beverly? She started spotting after menopause,

and she had ovarian cancer. I remember it as if it were yester—
"

"Ms. Stone. You're pregnant."

"W-w-w-what?"

The conversation speeds up.

"You're pregnant."

"No, no, no, no, no. I can't be. I'm forty-seven."

"It happens." She has the nerve to chuckle. "Not often, but it can occur."

"But—but, I—I can't be. I haven't had a period in, I don't know, thirteen months? Last year you said I was menopausal."

"I said your missed periods could be due to your weight loss. If I remember correctly, you were separated from your husband at the time and had lost a great deal of weight. I mentioned the lack of a period could be due to your weight loss or menopause." The tip of her finger scrolls through notes on her iPad. "Here it is. Yes. Stress or possible menopause."

"But that was a year ago. What am I, an elephant?"

"You may have missed a period for a few months due to the weight loss. During that time, menopause might have begun. But even if periods cease due to menopause, we advise women to remain on a contraceptive for a year. Hormonal activity can continue and cause pregnancy."

"Doctor Morgan, I cannot be pregnant. My husband and I tried for years to have another baby. My youngest is fourteen. My God, my oldest is twenty-one. I can't be pregnant."

"I very much assure you, you can be and you are."

"No, no, no, I couldn't get pregnant. Then I was menopausal. Angry. Sweaty. The doctor I went to before you wrote that down." I lean toward her and tap her iPad, hard. She jerks her shoulder and swings the iPad away from me. I point. "Look through your notes, you'll see. He told me not to come back because I was so nasty. You get that way when you're menopausal. You don't understand because you're young."

"Ms. Stone, you're pregnant." She sets her iPad down and places a hand on my arm, gently. "I understand this might be shocking. Is there someone you can call? Is the father still in your life?"

"What kind of question is that?"

"It's fine if—"

"Yes, he's still in my life. I'm forty-seven. What do you think I do, sleep around? And wait." I close my eyes and shake my head. "He's not the father. There is no father because I'm not pregnant."

"You should give him a call."

"I can't call him. Are you crazy?"

"Ms. Stone, calm down. Everything will be fine. I think you should phone him."

"I can't. He's golfing. He's a professional golfer. What would I say? Nice job. You scored a hole in one with your putter?"

"Tell him you are pregnant with his baby."

"He'll think I'm delirious," I scream. "I. Am. Forty. Seven. Years. Old."

Black closes around me, and I think I'm fainting, then whammy, the doctor shoves smelling salts under my nose and I spring to attention.

I glance around the room at the pictures and contraptions. The doctor has called the nurse in, and four beady eyes centered under arched brows stare at me. Moments ago I was afraid of death. Now I'm terrified of life.

Turns out, when you are forty-seven—the P-word is every bit as frightening as the C-word.

Chapter Four - The office

This is the worst thing in the world.

I'm on my hands and knees, wiping up vomit. Cleaning the bathroom floor at work has become my secret rendezvous. Three days in a row now I've thrown up at the office, twice missing the toilet. Keeping this pregnancy from Blake and my kids won't be my biggest challenge. Blake travels often, and my kids would never expect me to have a sex life; they barely recognize I'm breathing. But hiding it from my nosy coworker, Agnese Rose Wilson, will be a different story.

Agnese works in the cubicle beside me. I returned to work at Bruno's Financing, a small financial firm located in the downtown area of Erie, a city neighboring my Fairview suburb, when Mr. Bruno retired and his son took over. I'd worked here years ago but quit when Delanie was a toddler. Last year, out of the blue, Mr. Bruno called me and asked if I would consider returning. Miraculously, the phone call came right about the time I'd decided I couldn't raise Mark's illegitimate child—yes, he had the nerve to ask me (another long story I'll skip for peace of mind).

Other than Agnese, I love the people I work with. The problem is our building. It's a historical catastrophe. The Bruno's business has grown but the number of bathrooms hasn't. Jack, the owner's son, hired a contractor to extend the back of the first floor, adding restrooms, but it has been a code enforcement mess.

Nine men share one bathroom and seventeen women share a second crowded, two-stall nightmare. Yesterday, Agnese, the boss's long-time, sixty-something employee, walked in on me, plugged her nose, and walked out.

She's going to be a problem.

I stand. I've done the best cleaning job I can do with Mark's old t-shirt. I keep a bag of them at home and brought a few to work. I pilfered his favorite ones. I find satisfaction using them to clean bathrooms after the shitty way he treated me all those years. Fitting.

I turn sideways and stare at myself in the mirror, wondering how long I can keep my pregnancy a secret. Mark will have a field day when he finds out.

The door swings open. "My God, Nikki, what is the matter with you?"

Of course, it's Agnese. She can't stand it if I'm gone from my desk for more than a minute.

"I have stomach problems. You know that."

"You need a better diet. You've always eaten poorly."

"Just because I don't gorge myself with red meat and potatoes doesn't mean I eat unhealthily, Agnese."

"Well, Rosy says if you are going to date Blake Anderson, you have to take better care of yourself."

I stare her in the eye and don't blink. She knows this is a sore subject between her and me: that she has an inside line to Blake. The edges of her lips twitch. She loves mentioning her namesake, Rutger Rosy.

Agnese's only sibling, a sister, named her youngest daughter, whom they call Rosy, after Agnese Rose, who was named for their grandmother, Rose. By some miracle, Rosy made it into Rutgers University. No one is sure how. She's thicker than sludge in an alley, but that's all Agnese's family talks about.

Rutger Rosy lives in Atlanta now. She dates a golf pro.

My luck.

If Agnese even suspects I'm pregnant, she'll tell Rosy, and Rosy will blab it across the golf community.

"How's that hemorrhoid cream working for you, Agnese?" I say, and her face falls into a frown.

I heard her whispering to her doctor on the phone last week and where normally I give people in the office their privacy, I'd crawl on my belly under an electric fence to gather crumbs of dirt on Agnese. Blackmail is not beyond me. I might need her dirt to tamp down mine.

Her big mouth springs shut, and I leave her staring at a proud, little wiggle to my walk as I exit. When I get back to my cubicle, there's a note on my desk. The boss set up a meeting with me for 11 am. I wonder why.

Don't tell me Agnese mentioned my belching to him already.

Part of the reason I'm throwing up every morning is those god-awful iron pills the doctor insists I take. First of all, they're large enough to gag a buffalo. Secondly, they're black and metallic tasting. And thirdly, they're constipating.

I shouldn't have thrown the hemorrhoid jab at Agnese. Karma could come back to bite me.

The first time a nurse handed me a package of those pills I asked, "What's this?"

"It's for iron. Pregnancy depletes a woman's iron reserves."

"So, what? I shove one up my butt?"

"No." I remember her disgusted expression. "You swallow it."

"This?" I broke open the packet and held one in my fingers. "You expect one of these to slide down my throat?"

"All pregnant women have to take iron pills, Mrs. Grey," she'd responded.

"Do I wrap it in lard and sit outside the emergency room in case I choke?"

"Mrs. Grey, it's time for you to grow up." Back then, people weren't as hell-bent on socially acceptable customer service. "You're having a baby. Taking a pill is the least of your crosses to bear."

At the time, I was an oblivious twenty-six-year-old, completely unaware of the journey my body was about to embark on. Exuberant about having my first child, I had no idea I was imprisoned in a baby-making machine over which I had no control. Then the vomiting began. The emotional roller-coaster ride. Constipation. Stretch marks. Backaches. Saggy boobs. Dental problems from calcium depletion. Uncomfortable, sleepless nights.

The pregnancy memories flood me, and I'm unable to concentrate on my work. I sit doodling stick mammas with bulging bellies and twig babies with bonnets, a pile of unfinished work beside me. Since the doctor first spoke those frightening words, "You're pregnant," I have been wallowing in disbelief and self-pity, blocking the memories of the actual pregnancy.

The magnitude of everything hits me. I'll have to live through another nine months of hell.

At forty-fricken-seven.

I begin this snotty, ugly cry about ten-thirty. I hold a hand over my mouth, so no one hears me, and slump over my desk, so no one walking by sees me and suspects something's wrong.

I'm pregnant. I'm really pregnant.

All of the plans I've been dreaming about for the past year crowd into my head around my predicament.

"You can travel with me," Blake had said. "Meet me for long weekends. Come to California. Florida. The Georgia Golden Isles."

Blake insisted it didn't matter that I hated golf.

"You don't have to go to the tournaments. You can shop around them then meet me afterward in the evening." Blake isn't much of a social butterfly. "We can relax together, and when the tournament is over, the two of us can visit some of the sites."

Another thought jars me. Our trip to Europe.

Blake planned a trip to Venice, Rome, and Greece next year. The thought crossed my mind that maybe he wanted to make it a honeymoon. Or perhaps he planned to propose on a midnight gondola ride? Then again, there's a chance I am deluding myself.

I break into a sweat.

What if proposing never crossed Blake's mind? What if that European vacation was, well, just a vacation? Maybe he doesn't intend on getting married ever again, and I'll have to raise this child—alone. Or maybe he will marry me—feeling obligated then bitter, years later realizing he never loved me at all.

My mind takes off with this gust and sails straight toward Cape Fear. Instantly, I glance down the long hall of cubicles and dock my gaze on Lawrence Looney, who is, oddly, staring back. I look away.

Lawrence, not Larry—he detests that nickname because kids called him Looney Larry in grade school—is a forty-year-old accountant who barely talks. He wears thick glasses, sports a bald spot between two patches of hair over uneven ears, and weighs about ninety-nine pounds with his parka on.

Lawrence-not-Larry's wife, Lena, got pregnant before they were married. She was twenty and Lawrence was twenty-one. They married and raised two kids, Laura and Lawrence Junior. (People refer to them as the L family for more than their names.)

Last year at the office Christmas party, Lawrence admitted he had miserably fallen out of love with Lena and doesn't know what to do.

"She's a good woman. How can I leave her?" he asked me after three martinis. I had to drive him home and walk him to his front door, where, sadly, Lena had hung a large, shiny L.

That could be Blake. Blake could end up a Lawrence-not-Larry.

I sniff and wipe my nose because blowing it would broadcast to the office I'm crying. I try but can't shake the thought that Blake will be forced to marry me. He'll stay with me forever because I'm not a cheater, and he said he would never have left his wife for anything other than her adultery.

A sob escapes me, and I swat a hand across my lips. How can I do this? Trap him? He'll be like Lawrence-not-Larry. Start drinking. Stop coming home. Overstay his welcome at office parties, drunk and depressed.

This is the worst thing in the world.

Whimpering at my desk chair, I decide I can't tell him. I'll be sweet and kind and hopefully, if I'm a perfect girlfriend, he'll fall in love with me—really in love with me—and ask me to marry him before he finds out I'm pregnant.

I wipe my eyes and stop sniffing.

Yes. This I can live with.

I'm losing weight because I can't eat, so I can hide any baby bump for two more months. That should be time enough to prove my marriage-worthiness.

"Nikki!" I nearly jump out of my chair when Agnese yells over the cubical wall.

"What?" For once I've barked as loud as Aggie.

"Aren't you supposed to be meeting with Jack?"

I've been so caught up in my pregnancy, I've forgotten my meeting. I grab a pen and legal pad and scurry away. It's ten after eleven by the time I arrive.

"I'm sorry I'm late. I had some pressing issues, and time slipped by me." That's not really a lie.

"You're fine. I know we've overworked you lately. Come in and sit." He closes the door behind me.

"Listen, Nikki, you've done a great job in the past year."

It sounds as if he's laying me off.

"Thank you."

"You've really stepped up."

"I try hard."

"You finished the financials for the Rockwell account last weekend. And last month you spent an entire weekend wrapping up another."

"The Carson account."

"Yes. That's it. One of our largest."

"I didn't mind, honestly."

Blake had been out of town both weekends, so working at home hadn't bothered me. God knows my kids would never notice.

"Well, we've appreciated your dedication." He squirms in his seat. "There's something I need to tell you."

Here it comes.

He's trying to let me down gently. Business must be bad. The weakest links must go.

"Jerry is leaving."

"Jerry?" My voice hits its highest possible pitch. "Jerry Conway? Is leaving?"

I thought Jerry was a lifer. He's worked as the CFO for the Brunos for thirty-three years. They love him. He's like family.

"He's retiring. He and the wife bought a condo in Florida. He'd like to leave by the end of the year. He'll stick around until then to train someone new."

"Oh, he's going to be tough to replace. Clients trust him. The staff loves him."

"And that's why I've called you in."

"Me?"

"I don't think you realize how well-liked you are here, Nikki. Your work is impeccable, and you treat your clients and coworkers with respect and kindness."

"I think Agnese would beg to differ," I say without thinking, then immediately backpedal. "Oh. I'm sorry I said that."

Jack bursts into a laugh. "And that's the other thing we like about you. You're honest to a fault. You're right about Agnese. I don't think she likes a soul in this office, but she's a good bookkeeper. We overlook her shortcomings."

"She is good. I'll give her that. But what do you need from me then? My opinion? You have a lot of exceptional candidates right here in the office."

"We do. We know that. But we'd like you to consider accepting the position."

For a moment I'm speechless. "Me?"

Never in my wildest imagination did I see this coming.

"Yes, we'd like you to take his place as CFO. Of course, this would be a substantial pay raise, but I hardly think it would be a great deal more work. You've already been working nights and weekends. We'll move Larry up to your position. He's not as personable but he's a production machine."

"Lawrence?"

"That's right. He doesn't like to be called Larry. See? You always think of everyone else. You work well with Lawrence."

"I do; he's a great guy."

"We hope you'll accept…" he yammers on while my nausea inches back into the room. I'm able to control myself for what seems like hours of him trying to persuade me to say yes. In the end, he stops pressing. "We wanted to give you a heads-up. We won't need your answer until the end of next month. Think it through, talk it over with your family."

I'm so blindsided I shake his hand and say goodbye three times before I leave.

The CFO position; he's offered me the CFO position—and now I'm pregnant. How can this be happening?

I leave his office happy and sad and so confused I can't complete any work for the remainder of the morning or the entire afternoon. By the end of the day on my drive home, the question of whether I'm capable of being a CFO has exhausted me. I decide I must talk to someone and head toward Evy's. I'll beg for one of his pep talks, and he'll help me garner the courage to accept this job. Convince me that I won't screw this up, too.

"Don't tell him you're pregnant," I warn myself. He'll for sure tell Bennett, and Bennett will tell Blake.

"Don't tell Evy you're pregnant. Don't tell Evy you're pregnant," I chant over and over, all ten miles to his house.

Chapter Five - The tattletale

"I'm pregnant," I say when Evy opens the door.

Erroneously, I convinced myself I could limit my conversation to the new job offer, but as soon as I see Evy's face, I hurl the still-decomposing skeleton out of the closet at him in record time.

"When I said you were a good mother the other day, I meant it in the past tense." His thin, little lips squish together. He flanks his face with the palms of his hands, leans, and shouts through his makeshift megaphone. "As in, you are too old to have a baby."

"Sh." I grab his arm and shove him inside. "Where's Bennett?"

"Not home. Why?"

"You can't tell him."

"I won't. I'm 110 percent sure you're deluding yourself. Go sit down. I'll get coffee."

I slap a hand over my mouth and choke down a dry nothing because not a speck of food remains in my belly. My body's on a hunger strike.

I squeeze words out through my fingers. "No coffee. Please. Don't even talk about it."

After each pregnancy, I swore I'd never have another baby, not because of the pains of labor but because of the all-day sickness. It's not a morning thing. It creeps up day or night. I should have guessed something was wrong last week when the whiff of coffee began making me gag. I found out I was pregnant on Monday and by Tuesday, I'd switched from drinking four cups of coffee in the morning to sipping two bottles of Coca-Cola.

My morning routine has reverted to days of old: rise, run, shower, eat dry toast, swallow the horse pill, eat more toast, use all the fricking power I have to keep the pill down, throw up at the fourth stoplight on my way to work (it's a less-traveled spot) and examine the tarmac to make sure the horse pill hasn't unattached from my stomach lining.

Next, I enter a mini grocery store through its south-side door because I can't smell the coffee machines from there. I purchase two bottles of Coca-Cola. I sip one for the rest of my ride and hide the other in a file cabinet hugging the wall that separates Agnese and me. I munch on crackers, throw up, eat more crackers, and during lunch, I nibble toast and eat kale drizzled with olive oil—don't ask me why I like kale when I'm pregnant. Then I spend the afternoon yawning, the nausea resurfaces, but I hold off throwing up until I'm home cooking dinner for Gianna.

Only two-hundred and some days to go.

Fortunately, I'm the furthest thing from Gianna's mind these days, so she blocks out my retching easily.

"What do you mean, no coffee?" Evy is appalled.

I cover my mouth again.

"Don't depress me. You're the only person who likes coffee as much as me," he grumbles.

I gag, wave my other hand in the air, and give my head a shake, not too hard because any little tremor constricts my stomach. "Don't mention it," I manage to say.

He squeezes his eyebrows together. Normally, my entire world revolves around coffee, and Evy, more than anyone, knows this. I gag again and his eyes widen.

"You have got to be kidding me." He steps back, folds his arms, then snaps a hand out and waves it in my face. "You do not expect me to believe that at forty-seven-years-old you weren't practicing safe sex."

"Safe sex?"

"Yes, safe sex. You do remember what that is, don't you?"

"What? Stack pillows around my bed so I don't fall and break a hip? I didn't know you could get pregnant in the middle of menopause. Plus, Mark and I tried for years."

"This is so much more than I wanted to know about you, Naggy."

Dramatically, I saunter toward a couch and fling myself down. This is the death of my dignity. Everyone I tell will react like Evy, who has, in less than sixty seconds, experienced four stages of grief: disbelief, anger, depression, acceptance.

"Nobody gets pregnant at forty-seven." He's starting the stages over.

"Apparently, some women do, Evy. Do you have any Coke? And, please, you can't tell Bennett."

"Oh, darling, you're out of your mind if you think I can keep a secret as juicy as this from him."

I sigh. This is the worst thing that could happen: me blabbing my pregnancy to Evy. How do I get myself into these predicaments?

"Listen." I try to reason with him when he comes back with my Coke. "I'll be honest."

"That would be a first."

"The other day. I reminded Blake I was no longer dull and boring Nikki Grey. I was dull and boring Nikki Stone and he said—" I try to sound Blakey. "Maybe we can do something about that last name."

"Then what's the problem?"

"I don't want him to ask me because I'm pregnant. I want him to ask me because he loves me. I refuse to allow him to end up like Lawrence-not-Larry."

"That creepy guy at work who has a crush on you?"

Sometimes Evy is exhausting. "He's not creepy, and he doesn't have a crush on me but, yes, the guy from work who had to get married and fell out of love."

"He had to get married?"

"Yes."

"When?"

"At twenty-one, Evy. I told you this story."

"Blake is forty-six. You can hardly compare the two. He doesn't have Larry hair, either."

"He doesn't have what?"

"Larry hair."

"What in the world is Larry hair?"

"Androgenetic alopecia."

"What are you talking about?"

"Larry David, Lawrence-not-Larry, they have heads like a meadow mowed down the middle. Blake has a full head of salt-and-pepper hair."

"Seriously? You're talking about Lawrence's hair?"

"More lack of it. But if you're sure you're pregnant—wait—" He locks one hand on a hip bone. "Are you completely sure?"

"Yes."

"Doctor visit?"

"Three days ago."

"Blood test?"

"Yes, positive, and I'm throwing up every hour religiously. I'm pregnant."

Evy leans against the back of his chair, a contemplative silence washing over him. Finally, he says, "You must tell Blake."

My breath catches in my mouth, my cheeks bulge, and I blow air out forcefully. "You know I can't do that. It isn't in me."

He groans. His chest rises as he takes in a long breath, looking drained. "Naggy, for as long as I've known you, you've never had faith in yourself. You underestimate your value."

"You're right." I'm tired, too. Insecurity exhausts the minuscule strength I have whenever my life's pieces don't fall easily into the proper puzzle spaces. "But he'll feel obligated to marry me, and I wanted that to happen—I don't know— serendipitously."

"Blake loves you. Maybe this is destiny's wake-up call."

Life, existence, fate, and ideology consume Evy. I don't mind his idealism—until he forces it on me.

Philosophy bores me. The semester I took a class in college, I broke out in hives seven times worrying the professor would make me present my personal view on knowledge or truth. We recorded what we thought carpe diem meant on the first day, and Dr. Scarper said, "Let's discuss Descartes, Socrates, Emerson, and Nietzsche. Study Marx and Sartre. Hm? See how our definition changes."

The course was a mishmash of I exist, I don't, I'm important, I'm not. Our final exam had one question: What does carpe diem mean to you? I sat for an hour then wrote five words that summed up what I thought the professor wanted. "I think therefore I am."

He gave me an A. Wrote "brilliant" at the top of the test. Ridiculous.

Since then, I avoid philosophy like the dentist. But this one time, I have an ache that must be fixed.

"What does carpe diem mean to you, Evy?"

Quickly, he snaps his hands into his lap. His back straightens. Eyes, bulge. "What did you ask me?"

I've never had a philosophical moment in my life. Evy swims in them, so it's appropriate that when one finally surfaces in me, Evy is its recipient.

"You heard me."

In the many years I've known him, this is the first time Evy has looked insecure. He appears baffled beyond measure.

"To you. I really want to know. What does it mean to you?"

After the surprise in his eyes melts away, he answers, "Not important. What's important, Naggy, is what does it mean to you?"

College professors are all alike.

"I don't know. Be happy about the constipation and throwing up?"

He bursts out laughing and can barely control himself. I sit up with such glee that for the first time all week I feel happy.

"Pregnancy constipates you?" he squeezes out between laughs.

"No, the horse pills they make you take for iron do."

He doubles over. Getting Evy to roll into a belly-aching laugh is a hard feat to accomplish, so I rejoice in seeing him laugh so hard he's crying.

We toss constipation and carpe-diem jokes across the couch until our stomachs hurt, and I dry heave twice in his bathroom before I announce my unbelievable job offer. We discuss the pros and cons of my accepting the CFO position for over an hour then land smoothly back onto my pregnancy.

"I don't want you to tell Bennett I'm pregnant," I reiterate. "I have to do this my way. Maybe Blake does love me, and he'll never be a Lawrence-not-Larry, but I have to be sure. For peace of mind."

He doesn't respond right away, but about the time I'm ready to start nagging him for an answer, he closes his eyes and nods, "As you wish."

Then we hear the tires of a car rolling on cement, an engine coughing to a stop, and quick footsteps outside the screen door hurrying toward us.

Bennett steps in. "Hi, Nik."

I clam up and can't say a word. He gazes at me, at Evy, then back to me again. "What's up?"

Neither Evy nor I respond.

"Is something wrong?"

Evy clears his throat. "Naggy's having some problems."

Bennett walks across the room and sits down beside me. He sets his hand on my knee and shakes it. "I hope this isn't a problem with Blake. Is he treating you all right?"

I nod.

"Well, If I can be of help with anything, you know I will."

"She'll be fine," Evy says. "You know how she worries. She's had a job offer at work and isn't sure she should accept it or not. The CFO position."

"Nikki, that's awesome. You so deserve—"

"I'm pregnant." It rolls off my tongue like a mag wheel down a hill.

Chapter Six - The plan

The entire world will know I'm pregnant before Blake and my kids if I don't stop blurting it out like a foghorn.

I call my best friend, Jody, and cry on her shoulder. Next, I tell Val, three of my running buddies, and four high-school girlfriends.

At this rate, my pregnancy will be on tomorrow's evening news, which is a real possibility since the tournament Blake won over the weekend was huge. The major networks ran clips of their interviews with him, and local newscasters chatted him up on Sunday evening as I dressed and readied to pick him up at the airport.

The Erie terminal is small-scale, but two guys stopped him for his autograph while we waited at the baggage claim, and a third snagged him in the parking lot.

After we dropped his luggage and clubs off at his house, we drove to a little, out-of-the-way sports tavern, and the hostess beamed with happiness when Blake asked if his reservation was ready.

The owner magically appeared. "Mr. Anderson, yes, it is, and let me be the first to offer congratulations on your recent win."

When others in the room heard this, they began applauding. Blake's face turned a cherry red, and he nodded thank you to everyone as we followed the little man, who had tucked the menus under one arm and clapped the loudest. Once seated, he brought us a bottle of champagne on the house, and two more men stopped for autographs.

"This tournament must have been big." The wonderful thing about Blake is I don't have to put on airs with him. He doesn't care that all of my golf knowledge can fit into a thimble. "Will this win get you invited to more?"

"That's what I wanted to talk to you about." He lifts his champagne, swirls it around but doesn't drink, and personality number one, Scaredy-cat Nikki, forces personality number two, Confident Nikki, out of command.

Don't break up with me. Not now.

I lift my champagne to my lips, prepare to take a whopping gulp, then remember I can't drink. I set my glass on the table and push it away, unsure how I'll survive a breakup without the occasional sip or chug of alcohol.

He clears his throat and sets his hands on his thighs, sliding them up and down nervously.

I prepare.

Then he startles me with, "I'd like you to come to a tournament in South Carolina with me. I know you won't be able to stay the entire time, but if you could manage a long weekend, I'd love for you to be there."

"Oh." My mind does a 360. "I'd like that."

"Really?"

"Yes; I would."

"Can you take off work?"

"I'm sure Jack will let me. I have plenty of vacation and comp time coming."

"You do? How much?"

"Well, I told them I was saving the majority of this year's vacation for Europe next year, but I can spare a few days along with the comp time."

"That's right. Italy. Next May."

I can't read the expression on his face, but the tone of his voice says he's forgotten our trip.

"I'm sorry." Personality number three, Apologizes-for-everything Nikki, reacts. "Do you need to cancel?"

"No, but I might have to move the dates around."

"Because of golf?" These three innocent words come out wrong.

I never nag him about his passion, but my rapid response sounded much too snappy. In the deep dark crevices of my being, yes, I hate the sport, but I would never begrudge him his game. The emotion in my words springs from my fear he is falling out of love with me, not from his golfing

He hesitates and I'm tempted to say more but, smartly, I refrain. I've been down this road too many times, adding worse words to wrong words that trip awkward sentences and unintelligible paragraphs.

"Yeah." He lowers his voice. "I've been invited to several big tournaments."

"Like this coming weekend?"

"No, this weekend is the Columbus Charity Golf Classic. You said you'd go, right? We don't have to leave until after work on Friday, and we'll be home Sunday night."

"Oh, I thought we were going to a tournament."

"No. This is for fun, to raise money. You can golf, or, if you don't want to, you can go shopping and meet me at dinner afterward."

I shudder inside. I would be happy if I never gripped a golf club again for the rest of my life.

"The tournament I'm talking about is next month. We'd be there five nights," he continues. "I'd love for you to come. It's in Hilton Head. Have you been there?"

I release the tension in my shoulders and relax, happy he isn't breaking up with me or pressing me to golf this coming weekend.

"I spent a night there on my way to Florida and loved it," I lie.

Hilton Head isn't my favorite place. I rode a bike around the island with Mark once, and a pit bull galloped up behind me and took a chunk out of my butt. I swear Mark told the intern who stitched me up to go easy on the Novocain.

"Come. Take off work." He squeezes my fingers.

The thought of my job offer runs quickly past me. This is our slow time at work, so a few days off shouldn't be a problem. Delanie and Hux are home to keep an eye on Gianna.

"I think I can. Yes, I'm sure I can."

He's so happy that he leans across the table and kisses me on the lips.

"That would be great. We could rent bikes. Ride around the island."

Wonderful.

"There's a lot I have to tell you," he says, but the waiter interrupts to take our orders, and though Blake's sparked my curiosity, there isn't another second we can talk with the myriad of well-wishers stopping at our table. Men come and go, chat with him from side tables, even hail congratulations from across the room as a barrage of muffled golf conversations ricochet from table to table. Twice, women mosey over and introduce themselves, congratulating him, batting their fake eyelashes.

Do they not see he has a date?

In the middle of dessert, my nausea resurfaces, and I rush to the ladies' room, dash into the last stall, and hastily throw up while no one is there. Just as my stomach begins settling, I hear the rattle of the door and the click of heels against tile, and I hold my breath, hoping the women entering won't realize I'm there. One woman squeaks open the door to the first stall, and the other clunks what sounds like her purse onto the sink then rustles through it. I hide in my stall, holding my breath, willing myself not to gag.

"He is so good looking," the woman at the mirror says when the sound of the toilet flushing quiets. "Who is that woman he's with?"

"I'm not sure."

Are they talking about Blake?

"Bill says he's divorced. He was in a real slump for a few years after he and his wife broke up, but this tournament sent him back up the ranks. Bill doubts he'll stay in Erie."

"He might if he's dating someone here."

"I bet he has more than one girl."

"I don't know. He looked pretty smitten with her."

"They all look smitten before they get laid." The woman hesitates, smacking her lips as if she's applying lipstick. "He's a golf pro. Back from a big win. By tomorrow morning he'll have gotten what he wanted from this one and be off chasing some other dumb, size-two blonde. Bill says there's a rumor he had a mistress all along and—"

The other lady turns on the faucet and drowns out the rest of their conversation. They exit, I unlatch the lock on my stall, and sidle toward the sink. I'm shaking when I wash up. I can't imagine Blake had a mistress. He swore he had been faithful to his wife.

You trusted Mark, too.

Coincidentally, I'm clad in my new size-two skirt, and when Blake stepped off the plane earlier this evening, he asked if I could spend the night with him. He has to be at the golf course by five tomorrow morning but, of course, I could make myself comfortable, sleep in, and leave for work from there.

Is this woman right?

My mind chugs along, wandering over the past few months, wondering if what we have is casual. He's out of town a lot, and I suppose he could be dating women elsewhere. We've never proclaimed exclusivity, but we see so much of each other it should be assumed. Right?

I jump back and forth, afraid I've built our relationship into something bigger than it is. He seems devoted, but could he be concealing some hidden affair? Like Mark did?

My head spins and suddenly, I want to go home. In the thirteen months we've dated, I've never felt this way, wanted to distance myself from him, but I'm tired and pregnant and self-conscious and I can't survive another bad relationship. Not now.

"My house, then?" He asks when we are in the car.

"Would it be okay if you took me home?" I don't look at him.

"I thought the kids were gone tonight?"

I don't want to be anyone's fling.

"They are, but I'm not feeling well. I've had some stomach issues since you've been gone."

From his reaction, I can't tell if he's worried or disappointed. In my head, that woman's voice goads me. *"They're all smitten before they get laid."* My decision to go home strengthens.

"I'm sorry," I add.

"That's okay. I understand."

We're quiet for the remainder of the ride. When I get out, he walks me to the door, his chivalry weakening me. I have to force myself to resist the urge to invite him in. I'm convinced I need time away from him, so I can evaluate our relationship. I don't want the father of my child to be a fling.

"So, we are set for both Columbus and Hilton Head, right?" he asks on my front porch.

"This weekend, yes, but how about I let you know Tuesday on Hilton Head. I'll confirm it with Jack. He'll be back in the office then." I don't know why I'm suddenly unsure if spending five days away with him is a good idea. I'll see how this coming weekend goes then decide.

He sets a hand on my arm and leans to kiss me goodnight like a perfect gentleman. I swing my head, and his lips land on my cheek. He lingers for a while, and I wonder if he's hoping I'll change my mind and invite him in.

"I hope it works out and you can go. I'd like you to come," he says.

"Me, too. Bye," I force myself to respond.

"See you." He backs away, offering a weak, little wave before he heads to his car. I watch him drive away.

When he is out of sight, I change into comfortable clothes and make myself a big bowl of ice cream. I pour lots of chocolate syrup on it because, well, I'm probably going to throw it up anyhow. I spend the remainder of the evening with Furgy, the television set, and my ice cream toiling over what to do about my life. I search the channels for some life-revealing

a pappardelle and lamb sauce better than Rachael Ray. Blake loves a good meal.

I sit back to consider my list. It needs pizzazz. What can I do to impress him so beyond belief that he wants to spend the rest of his life with me?

The answer hits me. He needs more than a partner to spend lazy afternoons, long weekends, and warm evenings with. He needs a soulmate. Someone—he can golf with.

Oh, how I hate golf, but...

I write "dust my clubs off" in capital letters. Blake and I will ride the green fairways in his EZ-GO golf cart. The perfect little couple cruising off into the sunset.

Oh, yeah. With a baby in tow.

Chapter Seven - The first

Firsts make me shudder: First fifth-grader to start my period, first lunch (alone) in middle school, first traffic stop by a police officer, first marriage, baby—first moments at a national pro charity tourney.

The golfers and guests meandering up and down the grounds resemble the fairways: tailored, trim, and showy. These are affluent people who never hide their status—golf pros, politicians, philanthropists, capitalists—aristocrats. Bennett forewarned me of their snootiness, but nothing could have prepared me for the arrogance hovering over the greens.

I'm at the Columbus Charity Classic, a little sorry I agreed to come and still debating whether I'll go to Hilton Head in three weeks. My breasts have grown to gargantuan proportion. I barely see the ball at my feet when I tee off. By then, Blake will notice and begin asking questions.

Plus, I'm not fond of these people—especially Agnese's niece, Rosy.

I stomp to the second tee, pondering how Blake fits in this hoity-toity golf world. I remove my number one wood, not caring how short or far the hole is, set a tee in the ground, and swing, barely connecting. The ball rolls fifty feet and stops. I shove my club back in my bag and watch the next two women in my foursome send their balls soaring down the fairway. When Rutger Rosy removes a club from her bag, I spot a man with a camera setting up a tripod under a tree.

"What's that guy doing?" I ask her.

"You'll get used to it." Rutger lifts a hand and waves. The photographer fumbles with his camera and snaps a picture. "Give them what they want, and they leave you alone."

I make eye contact with the man, and he raises his hand. I smile and nearly wave but then realize he's motioning for me to get out of the way. I'm blocking his view of Rutger.

What does she have that I don't have?

I toss her a good, long girl-to-girl stare.

Everything.

She's wearing a pink blouse, a tight white skort that flaunts her long slender legs, and cute little white gloves embroidered with pink flowers. Her brown ponytail bobs behind two broad, yet thin, perfectly squared shoulders. She sports an eighty-dollar visor, cat-eye sunglasses, and a diamond-edged cable bracelet that falls loosely over one wrist. Everything about her screams "I love attention." She wiggles her cleats into the grass and readies to swing with a provocative jiggle of her derriere.

I can't believe I'm lowering myself to befriend her.

"Nice shot," I blurt out after she swings. I don't care for the woman, but I can't deny she's an exceptional golfer.

I stand alongside two other women, watching Rosy's ball land smack dab in the middle of the lane, twenty yards from the hole.

"Perfect execution," wife number one says. Her name is Carla. She's blonde-haired and blue-eyed like me, except tailored and neat, as if she stepped off the cover of a magazine.

"Who's your instructor?" Wife number two, Catherine, asks. She is a mirror image of wife number one, only bluer eyes, thinner waist, longer legs—and she's not as nice. She's scolded me twice already, reminding me to call her Cat. "You've improved immensely, Rosy."

We're playing on a practice course two miles away from the three main tournament courses. Pockets of amateur golfers chat and swing in foursomes around us while the executives with beaucoup money pay hefty sums to rub elbows with upcoming and retired pro golfers on the main courses. Later, everyone will dine on exquisite food prepared by world-class chefs, and local philanthropists have planned a Chinese auction, of which the proceeds are donated to some deserving charity I can't recall the name of.

But for now, I trudge down the fairway with three women who are annoyed because I'm not as good as them.

It's been four days since I devised my plan to win a proposal from Blake. I visited a driving range with Evy after work on Wednesday and Thursday, but my crash practice did me no justice. By the time I chip and putt my way through the second hole, I'm behind by five strokes.

"You're up, Nikki," wife number two, Catherine, says when we step up to the third tee.

Catherine (I refuse to call her Cat) and Rosy are friends. This morning they scurried toward each other, embraced excitedly, then stood off to the side snickering at the tournament organizer's outlandish plaid golf pants. Rosy introduced me to Catherine when I was forced into her foursome, and although that was barely an hour ago, she already sounds annoyed when she croaks my name.

I lumber to the tee box, and it takes me three tries to get the ball to stay on top of the tee. I spread my legs apart as Blake instructed me to do, grasp my club and swing, but I forget to keep my eye on the ball and miss.

"You have to count that as a stroke," wifey two goads.

"I know," I reply curtly. Then I add, "Catherine."

"Well, you didn't count your missed swings on the first hole." I'm sure she's rolling her eyes behind her shades. "And I told you. Call me Cat."

I'm in position, ready to swing, but I stop and bounce her a gaze. "Are you finished?"

She doesn't respond. Instead, she turns her back to me, laughing.

I swing again and, of course, I miss.

"Keep your eye on the ball," wifey one, says, and I don't have the faintest idea if she is being nasty or nice, but I do what she says and hit the ball fabulously hard. I watch it sail off to the right toward a gathering of people on the fifth hole.

"Fore," I scream.

Heads duck, my ball lands, and everyone averts a head clunker. After the other three smack their balls here and there but, at least, on our fairway, we gather our clubs and saunter toward our balls.

"Nikki," I hear and turn to see Rutger Rosy following me.

The holes on either side of us sport pockets of men watching her waltz my way. I step toward her, attempting to imitate her gait, demurely avoiding eye contact with any of the onlookers. Not that anyone looks my way when the bombshell is in motion.

"What are you doing?" she asks quietly.

"What do you mean what am I doing? I'm golfing."

"Do you know you had everyone ducking on the thirteenth hole?"

"What?"

She points to the left. A band of golfers is gathered on the fairway opposite the side where my ball has landed. "You have to give them a directional shout."

"I do?"

"Yes, let them know the ball isn't sailing toward them. It's common courtesy."

"I've never heard of that."

She lets out a hard sigh. "Honestly, I hate beginners, but only because you're from my hometown, I'll be nice. Yell 'fore' in the direction the ball is going and if there is a hole on the opposite side, you must turn their way and immediately yell 'play,' otherwise you're stopping everyone on the entire course."

"Really?"

"Welcome to the big leagues." She sighs and waltzes away.

For the next fifteen holes, I'm careful to yell 'fore' then 'play' at least twenty-five times. I'm so tired of swinging my club and chasing my ball that an urge to pack up and head to the hotel strikes me long before I finish the eighteenth hole.

While the women in my foursome are evil, laughing at every bad swing I take, others on the course are kind and compassionate. Men appear out of nowhere when I lose a ball in the woods or drive it onto a parallel fairway.

Afterward, at the clubhouse, I steer clear of Rutger. I gather my food and sit at an empty table waiting for Blake, who's still golfing. Several gentlemen join me, and my table fills quickly. When Blake arrives, he can't find a seat near me; not a single chair remains at my table. I'm surrounded by golfers—all men.

Blake stops to kiss me on the cheek; none of the men offer to move, but a man at the table beside ours waves him over. He moseys toward him, sets his dinner down, and winks at me as he takes a seat.

What began as kindness on the golf course has trickled over to the dinner. I'm not sure if people are treating me sweetly because I am Blake Anderson's girlfriend (not fling!) or they're hoping I am an avenue to Rutger Rosy. Honestly, I couldn't care less why. I'm tickled. I haven't had this many men gather around me since my college days. Maybe God has taken pity on me, and Blake will be a tad jealous and pop the question sooner rather than later.

With this thought, a flutter of excitement rises from the pit of my stomach and climbs to my shoulder blades. I square them.

Oh. Maybe that's the reason for my sudden popularity. My enlarged chest from my pregnancy. Is that what's drawing attention? I don't care.

I roll my shoulders back farther and flirt a little with my new golf friends. Loudly. I'm hoping Blake surmises I can be popular like Rosy and the other golfers' wives. That I'm important like them. Like him.

Later, after the dinner ends, we stroll toward the hotel holding hands in the warm night air. The moon rises over the tops of the trees. Its hazy light falls onto the path before us, and tiny footlights cast rectangular designs at our feet as we snake around shrubbery and trees decorated with accent lighting. Soft music is piped in, classical notes sounding from hidden speakers. Nothing could be more romantic and perfect.

"Nikki," he says. "I have to ask you something."

OMG.

Has adding golf to my plan worked? Is he about to propose? So soon? I'm pleased as pink at myself for deciding to give golf a try. If he asks me, I can tell him about the baby, not too quickly like I did with Evy and Bennett, but slowly, considerately.

I gaze into his eyes. Prepare myself. He's smiling. Wait. He's almost laughing. Would a man laugh while proposing?

"Ask me anything," I say, still hopeful.

"Why were you yelling foreplay throughout your golf game?"

"Because Rosy said—" I stop. "Wait, what?"

"Rosy? Did she say something to you?"

OMG.

The blood in my veins speeds up. My nausea heightens. I panic. "I wasn't yelling foreplay. I was yelling fore and play."

"Foreplay."

"No, no, no, no, no. Rosy said after I yell fore in one direction, I had to yell play in the other. You know. To the other side of the fairway where my ball wasn't headed. Let them know they could play on."

"So." He's trying hard not to laugh. "In essence. It came out as foreplay."

Blake has to stop. He can't hold it in any longer. He bends and laughs so hard he must wipe away tears. When he's done guffawing, he pulls me close and kisses me long and hard.

"Have I told you lately how much I love you?" he asks. He laughs again. "I suggest you don't listen to Rosy anymore."

From there on, the weekend slides right downhill and ends up in one of the worst gutters of my life.

Chapter Eight - The regroup

Bennett is doubled over laughing and Val is crying. On the chair between the two of them, Evy sits as still as a block of marble, his elbows chiseled into the kitchen table and his chin cradled in clasped fingers.

"You yelled foreplay," he says calmly, as if he suspected nothing less of me.

"Yes."

"Why would you do such a thing?" Val manages to squeak out.

"I assumed it was golf lingo. I was being careful."

"Careful?"

"Earlier, people laughed at me because someone mentioned the back nine were slick, and I asked what kind of music they played."

Again, laughter overpowers the room.

It's Tuesday evening, and Evy has invited Val and me and our families to dinner because Val's husband and Blake are working late. The three of us are rarely alone together these days. For years when the kids were little, we spent every Monday, and then some, together. Two other neighbors would join us, sweet-hearted Jody and slippery-tongued Ellie. Jody moved to the state of Washington, and Ellie's spending the summer carting her two kids around to soccer tournaments. They're hard to replace, but Bennett's doing his best. He fits in nicely.

Our kids are outside in Evy's back yard, playing cornhole. Their laughter floats through the open window, warming our evening's ambience. Despite the age difference in our children, our unwavering friendship has spilled onto them like a refreshing glass of lemonade in hot, clammy weather. Evy's daughters served as Gianna's sounding board, and Val's oldest became Delanie's emergency, only-a-text-away friend when Mark moved out of our house and in with his other daughter.

We four adults are inside drinking wine and lemonade, laughing like old times. The moment is uplifting. We've been through a lot this past year: marriage, divorce, sending kids to college, and missing our friend Gibraltar Jody, our rock. But we've settled back into a comfortable spot in the world of friendship. Surrounding yourself with people you can tell anything to, comrades you are seldom embarrassed around, soothes the soul.

"So you yelled fore and then play throughout the entire first game." Evy cups an elbow in one hand and tilts his head, studying me.

"Yep." I chomp on an ice cube from my lemonade and grab a cracker from the little plastic bag that is forever perched near my wrist these days. I refer to it as my nausea satchel. "I hollered foreplay up and down fifteen fairways."

"Only fifteen?"

"I was on the third hole when she told me." I shove a cracker into my mouth.

"How can one human being be so intelligent yet so wickedly gullible?" Val asks Evy.

"I work hard at it," I answer for him.

"You sound annoyed," he says. "You're no longer invisible. I thought that's what you wanted."

"I was hoping people would notice the good in me."

"That optimism is based on a faulty premise," he goads.

I frown and Val asks, "You say a barrage of men swarmed around you at dinner?"

"Indeed, they did." I sip my drink to wash down the dryness of cracker crumbs. "Several of those wonderfully kind gentlemen asked if they could take me outside and show me their putters. I thought there'd been a run on discount clubs."

Now Bennett sets his forehead on the kitchen table, gasping for air. We may have to call an ambulance. He's blue.

"Then the next day you drove a golf cart into a pond?"

"Yes, I did, Evy, because I wondered how I could ever replace my new nickname, Foreplay, so I drove a cute little cart into the edge of a pond. It wasn't fully submerged, but they had to tow it out."

"Marvelous, darling. Full steam ahead on that garner-a-proposal plan of yours."

Rutger Rosy has stalled my plan of impressing Blake with my marriage-worthiness. I'm in damage control mode.

"How did you drive a cart into a pond?" Val calms down to ask.

"It was hard, believe me. But my new friend, Rutger Rosy, went to great pains to help me out."

I'm beginning to think Rosy has the hots for Blake. Why else is she sabotaging me?

"The fake-boobs, silicone-lipped model who has Erie connections?" I love Val.

"Yes. She's a golf groupie. Moves through men like Joey through dogs."

"Who?"

"Joey Chestnut, the hot dog king," I explain to Val.

"Is she Agnese's granddaughter?"

"Niece," I correct Evy. "Rutger Rosy."

"Ah, yes. I remember her. The Rutgers wild card. No one knows how she got in. She's always at the center of the tournaments. Cameras love her."

"Yes, well, she's got a thing for me that's for sure."

"How did she goad you into driving a golf cart into a pond?"

"She asked me to help out and drive a cart back to the clubhouse. She said 'go on ahead' but 'make sure you give it enough gas to climb that first hill' because people had been stalling there all day. So I did, I gave it gas. She drove the cart behind me, and she rings me right when I swing around the corner. I take my eyes off the path for a minuscule second, grab my phone, and I'm in the drink."

They roar.

"Life's all about timing, Naggy. Perfection takes an attempt or two."

"You can say that again." I think of my perfect girlfriend plan.

Magically, Evy mentions it. "What's the next step on your plan?"

"Oh." I perk up, reinvigorated. "A regroup. I'm cooking dinner this weekend for Blake and his dad. Did you know your father is coming to town, Bennett?"

Bennett's face goes blank. "Have you met him?"

"No, why?"

His baffled expression alarms me.

"He's—how do I put this kindly?" Bennett drums his fingers on the table and rolls his gaze toward Evy. "Spacey?"

"Yes, spacey." There is no concern in Evy. "He'll love you, Naggy."

I ignore him.

"That's odd. You and Blake are so—in the moment." It's hard for me to believe their father could be flighty.

"We aren't like either of our parents."

"Thank God," Evy mutters and Bennett shoots him a frown. Caught, Evy returns a grimace then raises his voice. "You'll get along with daddy. Steer clear of mummy when she docks."

I have not an ounce of concern over Blake's "mummy." She's a do-over who spent the last eleven months circling the world in a yacht with her second husband. I'll worry about her when she's a mile from port.

"So. Think your dad will like me?"

While Bennett debates this question with chin raised and eyes to ceiling, Evy jumps in. "You'll get along fabulously, darling." I don't like the twinkle in his eye. "Like Buffay and Tribianni."

Chapter Nine - The remote

While fate's stars scatter in every direction over the golf course, at home, they align above Blake's house perfectly. Mark has invited our three children to two separate baseball weekends. Wonderfully, one is this weekend when Blake's father is arriving for a three-day visit.

Although Delanie and Hux have savored somewhat of a chip on their shoulder over Mark's cheating and the divorce, Hux can't pass up a ballgame invite, and Mark's invited Delanie's boyfriend, so she's agreed to go, too. Gianna visits Mark more often than the other two. She's taken a big-sister role in Rosalee's life. I've encouraged this. Rosalee adores Gianna, and she shouldn't suffer for Mark's mistakes.

I want them to have a relationship with their father and Rosalee, not because I'm a big person, but because I'm happy with my life. If I hadn't met Blake, I'd be miserably jealous and lonely when my kids were with Mark.

Rosalee's mother passed away in a car accident, which, in essence, is how I found out about Rosalee. I presume (but you never know) that Mark will not have (or has had) any more children, so my three kids will be the only siblings she has.

Something I don't discuss often is my sister Barb and I had different biological fathers. Never did I refer to her as my half-sister. I grew enraged when someone else did. My biological father was in Barb's life, raising her, by the time she turned four. He adopted her by eight.

"You don't tell people that's not your real sister when you're adopted, so don't call her my half-sister," I'd argue with kids in the playground when I was little. My father didn't treat Barb any differently than he treated me. We were both his girls.

My children, however, have been thrust into a much different situation. They won't be raised with Rosalee, and she was born out of wedlock, which puts an entirely different spin on the situation. What I endured—finding out Rosalee was conceived during what I believed was a monogamous marriage—was rotten. There's no feeling sorry for a man like Mark, but my fear for poor little Rosalee is that someone will tease her about being "illegitimate." When that day comes, I want my kids to defend her.

I set a reluctant hand on my tummy as if the child inside me can read my thoughts. I strum caressingly, try to reassure him or her that their life will not be as complicated. He or she will have five much older siblings—my three and Blake's two. I pray they are close like my sister and me.

"My dad loves chicken." Blake's answering a question I've forgotten I asked. I drop my hand from my belly and glance at his smiling face.

This baby will be luckier than Rosalee.

"Perfect," I respond, a renewed excitement rising inside me. "I'll make something special. I can't wait to meet him. What time?"

We decide on seven o'clock, and I spend Saturday shopping, tidying up Blake's house, arranging fresh flowers in vases, concocting a chicken-divan dish that would impress Gordon Ramsay, and I win Blake's dad over within five minutes of his arrival.

Dinner ensues without a hitch. He raves about my dish, doles out three large servings, one-after-another, onto his plate, and an hour later heads to bed stuffed and happy. The evening is so perfect that I wonder what Bennett and Evy were apprehensive about.

Blake and I clean up and head toward bed ourselves.

I've been nervous about sleeping with him this weekend. I'm afraid he'll notice my changing body. But I don't have to work too hard to fend him off because I threw up twice during dinner. When he snuggles beside me under the covers, I announce my stomach is still upset, he says he understands, pulls me close, and drifts quickly to sleep.

In the morning, I'm so pleased with myself and how perfectly the weekend is progressing that I decide to make French toast and blueberry pancakes. Blake offers to run to the grocery store with his dad.

Excitedly, I jump in and out of the shower. In my haste, I've left my underwear in the bedroom.

Blake's house sits on a shady, tree-lined street with pockets of brightly colored flowers spaced evenly in between. It's an older neighborhood with perfectly manicured boulevards and lots of personality, but Blake's home, warm and lovely, needs some TLC. His large rooms are adorned with crown molding, cherry woodwork, and beautiful but drafty windows, which will eventually be replaced. The house's biggest drawback is the lack of a master bath. The main bathroom, however, is large, stately, and sits directly across from the master bedroom on the first floor, so when I realize my forgetfulness, I dart across the hall, rustle through my bag for my underwear, and scurry back to the bathroom.

"Nikki?" I hear a male voice.

I freeze, stopping naked in the middle of the hall. Paralyzed. Holding my underwear. I'm not sure why I don't run.

"I want to watch the *Today Show*." I glance over my shoulder, and Blake's dad is shuffling straight toward me. I move one arm across my chest, drop the hand holding the underwear to my lower private part, and curl inwards toward myself, covering as much as I can.

I wait for him to realize I'm naked.

"I can't get this damn remote to work." He gazes up. We make eye contact, and he continues striding toward me, his droopy flannel pajamas wrinkled around him, the heels of his slippers heavy on the floor. I smell tobacco. He must have stepped outside for a cigar earlier when I checked to see if they'd gone. "Every time the picture comes on the sound is off and vice versa."

When he reaches me, he shoves the remote into the hand of my arm that covers my chest, raises his chin, and gazes through the bifocals perched on the end of his nose.

"Which of these buttons do I press?" he asks, annoyedly.

This has to be a nightmare. Can he possibly not realize I'm unclothed?

"I tried the green one on that remote." Like a magician, he pulls a second remote out of a back pocket. Shoves it downward. I open my fingers and grab it without moving my hand. My underwear falls around it.

"I don't know how to work these contraptions." He nudges his glasses up his nose. "I pressed the cable and TV buttons. I'm sure that's what Blake told me to do."

"Could I—" I'm about to ask if I can retrieve my clothes, but he interrupts, turns sideways, and steps beside me, so we can both look down at the buttons. At this point, he can no longer see the front of me. "What do I press?"

I point with the tip of one finger. "You have to press this one first, Frank."

"Then which one?"

I hear the front door open. Frank doesn't. He's a tad deaf, so I'm hoping he's a bit blind, too. I point to a button just as Blake passes by the hall, smiling, a bag of groceries in his arms. He marches straight toward the kitchen and disappears.

"Then you press this one," I say, watching for Blake to reappear.

It takes a second but, finally, he backs up. His cute little "oh you're talking to my dad" smile is replaced by gaping mortification.

"Hi, honey." I smile. "Did you forget to mention your dad wasn't riding along to the store with you?"

He's dumbstruck.

"Could you help him with the remote?"

"Oh, Blake." Frank yanks both remotes from me. In his haste, he's grabbed my underwear, too. He hands it back and heads down the hall toward Blake, who's lost the color in his cheeks.

I give him a little wiggly wave of my fingers and dart into the bathroom, feeling unattractive, unamazing, and repellently plain.

This confirms every fear about my ordinary, dull existence. I'm unnoticeable—even buck naked.

Something has to change in my life.

CJ Zahner   67

Chapter Ten - The gold

The aroma of my chicken divan and strawberry pie swirls around Blake's kitchen and slithers into the open dining area of his family room. Three bottles of the best wines from the vineyards of a small town located twenty miles away, North East, stand tall on an antique buffet counter hugging one wall. A grand mahogany table adorned with a lace tablecloth, pearl napkin rings, and seven bone-china place settings shimmer under Blake's crystal chandelier. One thing I do well is plan a wickedly good dinner party.

Blake and his father are at the driving range for an hour of practice while I entertain our guests—Bennett and my friends. I've enlightened them regarding yesterday's episode: Frank's unabashed disregard of my body.

"Val, you can stop now." All have arrived except Val's husband, who works late and will scurry in at the last second. My naked-in-the-hall story has them in stitches.

The most magnanimous feature of my friend Val is that she owns this mischievously contagious laugh that hangs on like a fly on a racehorse. When you hear her, you want to jump up beside her, view the road through her eyes, and ride along. She and Bennett are stretched out on Blake's couch, laughing, but the volume of her voice triples his.

Val and Evy have been best friends for years. My best friend, Jody, and I, along with two other neighbors, Ellie, who is on the soccer furlough with her kids, and Reah, who has since dissed me, met at a neighborhood playground when our kids were little. Our personalities clicked.

Today, four of us—me, Jody, Val, and Evy—remain as close as four stacked sheets in the middle of a tightly-packed ream of paper, except Jody lives hundreds of miles away now and communicates via text and Facetime.

Our four personalities are the epitome of a melting pot. We are a swirl of bold, blended colors, bright and distinct, alike in intelligence, yet we prove opposites attract. Evy's disposition is as different from Val's as my attention span is to Jody's. Evy is a sober academic struck with dry humor, and Val is a burst of laughing gas. They feed off each other. And Jody's mind is grounded, while mine wanders in cumulous clouds. We reinforce each other.

Now that Bennett has turned our foursome into a fivesome, three of us—not Jody because she's too far away and too sensible—clamor to lock pinky fingers with him. Val's winning, which annoys Evy.

"But you weren't in your own house. How could you think running naked down the hall was okay?" Val asks. Bennett adds a good-point nod.

"I wasn't running naked down the hall. Look." I point and everyone leans to glance down Blake's hall as if they've never seen it before. "The bathroom is right across from the bedroom. Less than a second away."

Evy leans back in his seat. "Once again, timing is everything."

"Yes, it is. I didn't know whether to be appalled that Blake's father saw me naked or mortified that he was so unimpressed."

"Another boost to the ego." Evy raises his coffee cup to toast me.

"He must be blind. No one could miss those boobs." Val stares at my chest.

"He did. I'm pretty sure he elbowed one by accident."

Bennett has to leave the room he's laughing so hard, and he can't do it like a man. He crawls down the hall toward the bathroom on his hands and knees, crippled by hilarity.

"It's not that funny, Bennett." This is the first time I've become cross with him. A minute later he slithers back and apologizes.

"She's mad at your dad, not you," Val tells him. "He should have liked her saggy chest. He's old."

I gaze down. They've been tossing insults about my pitifully plain, unnoticeable body for the last fifteen minutes. I'm becoming self-conscious. "This pregnancy is rearranging me. I need a better bra."

"They sag?" Bennett asks Val.

"You didn't know that?"

"No."

These Anderson boys never cease to amaze me. "Bennett isn't like you and Evy, Val. He's not all about other people's flaws. He's nice."

"Wrong. He simply doesn't have access to the parts." Evy makes his way toward the kitchen. "More coffee, anyone?"

"Can you grab me a Coke?" I holler. I reexamine my chest, wondering how long before Blake notices my cup-size increase.

Sadly, the one time we women can count on being top-heavy is during pregnancy.

"Did you grow to this size with the other kids?" Val points at my chest. "You can't keep your pregnancy secret if they get much bigger."

"It was so long ago I don't remember." I fumble with my bra, shorten the straps and raise the cups.

"What did you say?" Bennett speaks lowly to Val.

"Boobs," Val answers, loudly. "They get bigger when you're pregnant."

"They do?"

Both Val and Bennett lean toward me for a better glance. Val inches uncomfortably close.

"Val, can you back off?"

She pays no mind, moving closer. "I'm betting he notices soon. You're blooming."

Her observation may be accurate. My imagination may be stalled on my voluptuousness, but the last time we made love, it seemed Blake couldn't keep his hands off my chest. I blush as if someone can read my thoughts.

I won't be able to keep this pregnancy from him much longer if we are sleeping together.

"What's next on your list?" Val retreats, backing away.

A few days ago, I attempted to impress Evy and Val by showing them my great-girlfriend, get-a-proposal list. Evy and Val are equally consumed with goals and objectives. Val, like Evy, has preached lists for years. They insist listing the good and bad about your life organizes the skeletons in your closet. Cleanses them, so you aren't coughing up dust from the past.

When my friend Reah cut me out of her life, Evy insisted I divide my friends into two lists, categorizing sketchy friends on the Friends Who Move Couches list (that name is another story) and true friends on the Friends Who Move Bodies list.

Val and Evy, along with sweet Jody, were at the top of my bodies list.

This I know to be true: these three will always laugh with me, never at me.

Sticks and stones alone don't hurt a person. Words, or the lack thereof, can cause as much pain. I continually lecture my kids on this subject concerning social media.

Facebook is more than a frivolous time-passer. It's a weapon with a sharp blade that cuts. My girls and I have been thrashed with both words posted and blatant disregard. When bad people come at you, it doesn't hurt nearly as much as when good people cold shoulder you.

Facebook allows good people the opportunity to hurt others. They flaunt their religious beliefs and holier-than-thou attitudes, cite scripture, post spiritual quotes, then shun someone with the scorn of Satan. They like and comment on anyone and anybody's posts, shower the masses with compliments and thumbs ups but ignore that one individual they're mad at. It's a "See, I'm good. I would never disparage anyone. I'm a child of

God" tactic. They hang their hats on the "if you can't say anything nice, then don't say anything at all" hook.

But sometimes, it's the things we don't say and the things we don't do that hurt others.

My ex-friend Reah who dissed me isn't a bad person, yet she decided I wasn't good enough for her and went out of her way to avoid me in person. As if that wasn't hurtful enough, she ostracized me on Facebook. She constantly liked and commented on my friends' posts to let me know she still loved them, just not me.

Her snubbing crushed me and my girls. My kids had grown up with hers, and suddenly our entire family was shunned—because I was unlikable.

It's sitting in the lunchroom alone, all over again.

Yet, life went on, and my girls and I weathered through with a little help from our true friends. Evy, Val, and Jody don't comment on Reah's posts anymore because they know she's hurt me. So regardless of how hard Val laughs or Evy teases or Jody scolds, I know they truly have my back. I can count on them—always—no matter what happens in life. Evy, Val, and Jody's names are embedded in my friends-who-move-bodies list.

Just as Blake's should be. He never demeans, criticizes, or judges. He accepts me as I am.

I wonder which list of his I'm on?

My self-doubt resurfaces. "I'm supposed to go to Hilton Head with Blake next weekend, but I don't know. I'm trying to stay off his bad Nikki list."

Bennett sobers up. "Evy, why do I believe this bad Nikki list has you written all over it?"

I'm sure Evy's convinced Bennett to concoct a list or two or three or five hundred.

"Oh, my." Val wiggles into her seat as if she's about to watch a Lifetime movie. Bennett and Evy seldom bicker. "Trouble in paradise."

"I have no control over your brother's lists," Evy retorts.

"That's because he doesn't keep lists," Bennett counters.

"Everyone keeps lists. If not physically, then mentally. Nikki's simply attempting to stay out of his subconscious atrocious-girlfriend registry."

"Registry? As in a girlfriend registry?" I jump in. "Is that for registering flings?"

"Evy, you're scaring her. Blake doesn't have other girlfriends, Nikki."

"No." Evy sips coffee. "Just subliminal lists."

"How do I stay off a list he isn't even aware he has?" I lament, then my gaze falls to my chest. "I could be watermelon-sized by the time we go to Hilton Head."

"For heaven's sake, tell him," Evy barks.

"Tell me what?" Blake steps out of the kitchen.

I can't say a word. I'm stupefied. How much has he heard? My cheeks heat up like coals. You could toast a marshmallow over me.

"She thinks she's ruined the chicken divan. She doubled the lemon juice and knows you hate lemon." Bennett's cool-headedness rescues me. "But it's fine. I tasted it. You can't tell."

Blake heads straight toward me, a can of beer in his hand. He sits and slides an arm around me. "She's too hard on herself."

They debate this issue in front of me as if I'm not here, but I am so caught off guard by Blake charging in, it takes time for my fear adrenaline to simmer. I don't speak. The conversation eventually progresses to another subject, and for once, I haven't made a fool out of myself by blabbering.

Because I'm exhausted from tirelessly cooking the past two days to impress Blake's dad, my quietness spills over into dinner, and it could be my imagination, but the less chatty I am, the more respect I command. Val asks me for recipes. Blake's dad and Bennett take turns complimenting my meal, and Evy, who usually torments me relentlessly, converses with me serenely.

As we finish dinner and dishes and gather for a nightcap (Coke for me. I tell Blake it has rum mixed in.), the others talk golf, and I chat even less. When Val brings up my pending CFO job, no one scolds or badgers me. They civilly discuss the pros and cons of my accepting the position. They don't realize I've hardly participated in the discussion, but because I'm talking less, they listen to me when I do speak.

An enlightening concept dawns on me: closed-lipped people often appear smart—intellectual.

One of my running friends, Wes, is painfully quiet, and no one wants to run alone with him because it's intimidating. You're forced to carry the conversation yourself, opening up the chance of saying something senseless to this genius of a guy.

A light ignites in my head. The true meaning of the law of averages, learned so long ago, slaps me.

Why haven't I realized this? Maybe Wes isn't a genius. Maybe he's simply quiet, and the people around him converse too much, risking the utterance of some idiotic statement.

If I talk less, my chances of lodging a foot in my mouth wanes.

This is brilliant. I can't believe it took me forty-seven years to realize quiet is gold.

I continue holding my tongue for the remainder of the evening, and Blake is sweeter to me than ever. Later, after our guests leave and he's asleep, I retrieve my phone and text myself to add an amendment to my great-girlfriend list when I get home: Quiet is gold. Stop chitchatting so Blake thinks I'm smart.

For the first time since I found out I was pregnant, I sleep like a baby.

Chapter Eleven - The proposal

Outstanding.

My quiet-is-gold plan amendment has proved to be outstanding. Blake has been so attentive that I'm certain he'll ask me to marry him as soon as he returns from his weekend away.

"Hi, Nikki." Lawrence interrupts my daydreaming.

I stop scrubbing, circle one shoulder to release its tension, and decide I'm due for a break. I toss my sponge and plastic gloves on the table where Lawrence is sitting and remove a Coke from the pocket of my apron. I sit down beside him, wiping sweat off my brow. Bagging garbage and cleaning tables at this fancy yet cafeteria-style dining room is work. I twist the lid and drink. Instantly, the Coke does its trick, settling my stomach. I've only thrown up once today. I'm volunteering at the Erie Golf Charity Classic.

Golf balls. I can't escape them.

"I thought you were going to Hilton Head," Lawrence-not-Larry remarks, drink in hand. He can't tear his eyes from my chest.

I'm close to getting a proposal, but regretfully, Blake hasn't asked yet, so I declined the Hilton Head trip. I've spent the last few weeks working extra hard, impressing him everywhere but in the bedroom. I cooked him multiple meals, cleaned his house, and kept my mouth shut to seem more intelligent. He'll ask soon.

"I decided not to go."

Every year, the Bruno family hosts a charity golf classic at a local golf course. I served food and picked up after dinner last year, so when I realized the classic fell on the same weekend as

Blake's Hilton Head tournament, I used it as an excuse. Blake was disappointed but I had no choice. I have to stop sleeping with him until he proposes.

"How come you hate golf so much?" Lawrence asks. His eyes haven't moved.

I stretch an arm, touch a finger to the bottom of his chin, and lift, severing the ménage à trois his gaze is having with my breasts.

"Because I'm not thrilled with sports, to begin with, but golf is possibly the dumbest game I've ever seen." I withdraw my hand and spread my fingers around my Coke. "Chasing a little white ball around with a stick? I can't imagine why a man would create such a game. Probably to drive his wife crazy."

Lawrence chuckles and I gaze at him carefully. He only laughs when he's drunk and, sure enough, he's inebriated. This is becoming a habit.

"Oh, Nikki, you're so adorable."

I lean away and stare at him. His gaze has once again fallen to my chest.

"I wish Lena could be more like you."

I slide my chair away from him, its legs screeching. "Lawrence, how many drinks have you had?"

"Three or four." He can't dislodge his eyes.

I reach over and push his drink away from him. "You're not driving, are you?"

Finally, I've distracted him. He slogs an elbow on the table, schleps a hand to his plastic cup, and chugs the remainder of its contents.

I sigh. I'm going to have to drive him home again.

"Will you two please stop chatting and come help?" Aggie interrupts. I check my pockets to see if she's planted a tracking device in my apron. There have to be three hundred people at this golf club, and the two of us are tucked away in a back corner. "What are you doing? The Chinese Auction is going on and as soon as it ends, we have to clean."

"Leave us alone," Lawrence says, confirming his lost sobriety. In over a year of working with him, I've heard him issue only a few brisk orders, mostly over the phone to his wife. "We're having a personal conversation, Agnese. Keep your big nose out of it."

"Lawrence," I say. "How about I fetch you a cup of coffee, and you sit here and sober up. I'll drive you home."

"Okay, Nikki." His mien turns sweet. He tips his empty cup and attempts to drink, glances into its bottom, and tries to stand. "I'll have one last drink."

"Not a good idea." I lean a hand onto his shoulder, guiding him back into his chair.

"Okay, Nikki."

"Wait here. I'll get your coffee."

"You are the sweetest woman I've ever met. I wish Lena could be more like you." He attempts to drink from his glass again.

"I'll be back."

On the way to the kitchen, Agnese chastises me for sneaking off with Lawrence, and I have to join in a golf conversation with Jack Bruno to unloose her from my heels. A few minutes in, I politely excuse myself, grab Lawrence a coffee, then spend the next hour thanking golfers and cleaning tables. Three times I see Lawrence sneak to the bar. When I finally return to the back corner, Lawrence's empty glass is nudged against a cold cup of coffee, and his forehead is kissing the table.

I help him to his feet and lead him out the front door. About the time he begins slipping toward the ground, Agnese steps beside us, arms crossed.

"A little help, please," I say.

She grabs his arm, and the three of us meander through the parking lot.

"Why don't you call him a cab? He's drunk."

"I'll drop him off. It's on my way home."

"He's made a spectacle of himself."

Lawrence straightens to attention, sways, then clumsily pats down his shirt. "You shouldn't talk to Nikki like that."

"You're drunk, Larry. Go home to your wife and kids," she hisses.

"Don't you call me Larry." Immediately he springs to anger. He jabs a finger at Agnese, makes contact, and she turns a shoulder, leaning away.

"Get your hand off me."

"It wasn't my hand. It was my finger." He twists his still-pointing finger towards the sky and jabs it up and down, a take-that motion.

"I could have you fired for touching me."

"Come on, Agnese, leave him alone," I say. "I'll take him home, and he'll sleep it off."

Lawrence-not-Larry puffs out his chest. "You should be more like Nikki. No one likes you. Everyone in the office loves her and hates you." He's slurring his words so badly I hope Agnese doesn't understand what he's saying.

"Lawrence," I order, "stop. You'll regret this in the morning." He staggers and I slip a shoulder under his arm to prevent him from tumbling over. "Try and stay upright."

I open the passenger door with one hand and nudge him toward the seat.

"Aw, Nikki, you're such a sweetheart. That golfer? You know." He attempts to put a finger on his chin but misses. "What's his name again?"

"Blake."

"That's it. Blake. He doesn't deserve you, that old Blake."

I help him into his seat while Agnese serenades us. "This is the fourth function in a row he's gotten drunk at. You aren't really taking him home, are you?"

"Yes, I am. Unless you'd like to."

I tug at his seat belt and lean across his lap to buckle him in. He puckers his lips and kisses my cheek. "You're an angel. Did anybody ever tell you you're an angel?"

"Thanks, Lawrence."

"Did he just kiss you?"

I shut the door carefully. "Listen, Agnese, he's going through a rough time. Can't you cut the guy some slack? This one time, have some compassion."

I leave her standing on the curb. She's talking to me while I slide into the car, slam the door, and back out of the parking space, but I can't hear her. Lawrence is singing some Irish song about a girl named Molly Malone.

I drive several blocks before realizing he has a tremendous voice. He belts out stanza after stanza in perfect pitch despite his drunkenness, slipping into an Irish brogue.

"Lawrence," I remark when he finishes. "I didn't know you could sing. You're fabulous. Have you sung professionally?"

"Nah, Lena and I used to book a few evenings at different clubs when we were younger, but we don't sing anymore."

"Oh." This is the first time he's mentioned Lena without being derogatory, so I try to coax more compliments from him. I'm not convinced he doesn't still love his wife. Mid-life thrusts the best of couples into slumps. "Lena sings, too? You must have been quite the duo. I bet she had a great voice."

"Lena was a fine singer. Auditioned in New York City for a part on Broadway. Won the understudy for the lead before we met."

"Lena?" I can't hide the surprise in my voice. "Was on Broadway?"

"Nah, the show only ran three months. The lead never missed a performance." He leans toward me and winks. "She was afraid she'd lose her spot. Lena was an unknown but had a better voice. She was something back then."

"Is that where you met her? In New York City? How romantic."

"Yeah, she was wearing a blue skirt. Had the best legs in the Big Apple. Better than the Rockettes'. And an adorable laugh. A contagious, wild laugh." He drifts back in time, quieting for a moment. Then he slides back into a drunken despair. "She never laughs anymore."

I attempt to wrench him back to happy memories. "I had no idea Lena hid such talent. She's so sweet, she'd never brag. She's always kind when she stops at work. Nice to everyone."

It's too late. He swings his head to face me. "But not like you, Nikki. She's not sweet and gentle and kind like you."

Not the response I hoped to arouse.

"You don't know me, Lawrence—"

"Yes, I do. You're an angel," he stammers. "Lena's old and frumpy."

"She is not."

"Yes, she is. She never dresses up. She goes to bed early."

"Lawrence, she has two kids. She works full time. Manages a house."

"But look at you." I gaze across the front seat. He's nearly drooling. "You're beautiful. So together all the time."

Evy was right. Lawrence does have a crush on me.

"No, no, you don't know the real me, Lawrence—"

"Yes, I do."

"I'm a space cadet."

"No, you're not."

"Can't keep my mind nailed down on anything. Half the time I don't know what I'm doing. The other half, I don't know where I'm going. I'd get lost on a racetrack."

"No, you wouldn't." A grin adorns his doting objection.

"Lawrence, did you ever hear the saying the grass looks greener on the other side?"

"The grass is always green by you, Nikki."

He's beginning to slump toward me. He might be passing out. I set a hand on his shoulder and shove him back into his seat. He places his fingers over mine right as I stop at a red light. I glance at him.

"If I leave Lena, will you marry me, Nikki?"

Apparently, I need to be more specific when I pray for a proposal.

Lawrence attempts to kiss my knuckles, misses, and kisses his own. "Be my wife, Nikki."

I yank my hand away, and he falls toward the space between us, bumping his face on my car's stick shift. Blood gushes out his nose. I reach to the floor of the back seat, grab a t-shirt from my stash, set it on his face, and ram him back into an upright position. The light turns green, and I hold him in place for half a mile then steer into his driveway and lean on my horn.

After a minute, Lena appears. I jump from the car, jerk open his door, and unbuckle his seatbelt.

"What happened?" Lena helps me get him out.

"Too much to drink. He smacked his nose on the car shift."

I hold the shirt to his nose as Lena and I help him into the house. Because he's bleeding so profusely, he can't talk and that's good. I'm afraid he's so inebriated he'll ask Lena for a divorce.

We plunk him into a chair, and Lena tips his head back and pinches his nose, applying pressure. In a few minutes, the bleeding subsides. She moves his fingers to his nose. "Hold tight, Larry. Keep applying pressure while I walk Nikki to the door."

One hand grasps his nose. His other slogs at the air, groping at nothing, and he mumbles indecipherable words as we walk away. I hurry out of earshot, afraid of what he's mumbling. When I step outside onto the porch, Lena follows me, closing the door behind her.

"He's always gotten nose bleeds. He'll be fine." She sets a hand on my arm and won't let go.

The night air seems disturbingly thick. Her fingers squeeze, but she remains silent. The hum of traffic in the distance drifts down her quiet street and hovers awkwardly around us. Finally, she blurts out, "How does Larry seem at work?"

That she calls him Larry baffles me. I pause, gaze toward the front door, and consider Lawrence's mental well-being of late. With so many pressing issues of my own, I haven't paid much attention.

"I don't think any different. He's always been quiet. A great worker, though. Jack Bruno mentioned how hard he works."

She bites her lip. Silver moonlight falls around her, and I see the remnants of a once striking face, now dappled with doubt and diffidence. An instant comradery strikes me.

"I'm at wit's end. He's unhappy, and I don't know what to do for him. I'm afraid we've grown apart."

I notice the dark circles beneath her eyes. Despite her fatigue, her weariness can't destroy the softness of her face. I've never noticed this in the past, my mind eternally stuck on myself, but Lena is fairly pretty. I gaze long and hard at her. She's quite attractive. And, clearly, she still loves Lawrence.

"Marriage is never easy." I set my hand on hers. "The ups aren't always as high as you hope, and the downs can be unbearably low, but if you love each other, you see it through."

"I don't know."

We release the grasp we have on each other. Lena folds her arms and raises her shoulders as if more than the evening chill runs through her.

"Have you gone to counseling?" I ask.

Mark and I tried counseling. A friend suggested a female counselor, Tracy, whom I love. I still see her once a month.

An idea pops. Counseling couldn't mend my relationship after Rosalee was born, but maybe there's hope for Lawrence and Lena. I pull my phone from my pocket. "What's your email?"

"My email?"

"Yes, I'm sending you the name of a wonderful counselor. She's helped lots of couples."

"But you and Mark—I'm sorry. That's none of my business."

My reputation precedes me. Agnese informed the entire office that my husband fathered a child by another woman weeks before I started back to work there. I couldn't expect anyone, even Lawrence, to keep that secret.

"Lena, Mark and I were lost. We didn't love each other. There's hope for you and Lawrence."

"Oh, well." Her glance bobs back and forth across the floor of the porch. "I guess we could try."

Timidly, she relays her email. I sing Tracy's praises, explaining how sweet and supportive she is, and I send Lena her contact information. I'm not one hundred percent sure I'm giving Lena good advice. If it turns out Lawrence doesn't love her, she's in for a rough time—I know.

I hug her gently before taking off down the porch steps.

"Nikki," she calls.

"Yeah?"

"Do you think—" She stops and I wait, squinting through the night's shadows. Despite the late hour, I see she's blushing. "Never mind. That's presumptuous of me. Go on. Thanks for dropping Larry off."

"No, wait. What do you need?"

Lena tugs at the ends of her hair. "Larry says you know how to dress. We saw a glimpse of you on TV at a golf tournament last week, and you looked stunning. Do you think—could you possibly take me shopping sometime? Larry suggested it once, but I felt uncomfortable asking."

She lets go of her hair and fumbles with the buttons on her blouse. She's hunched over, scrunching her shoulders inward. Her eyes blink bashfully.

If these two introverted souls don't belong together then there is no such thing as a soulmate.

"Lena, every time I've seen you, you look wonderful."

"Well, thanks but I'd rather look like you."

"I'm not sure why, but I'm always searching for someone to shop with. I have to run to the mall Saturday. I could meet you there." I don't have the heart to turn her down. While I'm not the most religious woman in the world, I do believe God guides us in the right direction. Maybe I'm meant to help them save their relationship. "Prepare yourself, though. I'm not the best dresser."

"Oh, but you are. Larry says the girls in the office love you because you're so pretty and so well dressed, yet you don't have a pretentious air about you."

"Thank you for the compliment."

"It's the truth."

"Then let me be honest. If my two headstrong daughters didn't help design my wardrobe, I'd be frumpy. Let's meet at, say, three? I'll try to remember everything they've taught me."

"That would be wonderful, Nikki."

I head home, impressed with myself. For once I'm not consumed by my own problems. It's nice to forget my woes and do something for someone else for a change. I turn on the radio and hum happily toward home. Then a dark realization hits me. Something I haven't thought about until right now.

OMG. I have to shop in the maternity department.

Chapter Twelve - The mulligan

"I love him but he's not my soulmate," admits the pretty girl with the round face. She speaks into the camera with confidence. Her fiancé sits beside her; his expression sags. He hurts, and my empathy soars.

Is that why Mark cheated? We weren't soulmates?

Ninety Day Fiancé is possibly the most frivolous TV show ever filmed, and I'm an idiot for being helplessly addicted to it, but there are advantages of watching. For one, my girls love the show, and I experience a comradery with them; we share our mortified reactions. Two, I gain empathy by witnessing the disparity in the lives of people living in third-world countries; someone's always trying to get a green card. Three, these ridiculous across-the-world romances make me feel better about my life. And four, believe it or not, its superficial footage of raw human emotion evokes questions in me.

Can a person have more than one soulmate?

I was goo-goo-eyed when I first met Mark. I told everyone I'd found the man of my dreams. My mother cautioned me not to get caught up in the spoony adrenalin of my new fling, but that's tough advice to follow in those first months. You've shined up your personality and whittled your wardrobe down to your best fits but so has he. Mark camouflaged his bad temper and flaunted the minuscule speck of gentlemanliness he owned, while I hid my flighty insecurities and ravenous appetite.

Back then, when Mark took me to dinner, I ate beforehand, selected the cheapest item on the menu, and picked at my food as if my stomach was the size of a pea. Concealing your flaws can be daunting. When we went to the beach, I held my stomach in for hours. In the car, I sat with my shoulders squared. I plucked my eyebrows and painted my toenails every other day. I yearned to impress Mark day and night—even years into our marriage.

Then I had kids. Self-grooming—inside and out—came to a screeching halt.

Blake and I are still swimming in the pool of initial affection. How do I know I won't realize five years from now that he isn't my soulmate? Like Mark. Or worse, what if he is mine, but he realizes I'm not his?

He flew home Monday and drove directly to my house. The kids weren't home from another baseball excursion with their dad, so Blake asked to spend the night. Unprepared for that question, I stammered then said yes, knowing I would have to do a song and dance later about not feeling well so he didn't expect more than a good night's sleep.

He cannot see me naked.

Fortunately, I'd been hard at work on my get-a-proposal plan. I had a grilled steak ready and waiting for him, a side dish of rosemary fondant potatoes, a Tuscan salad, and carrot cake. I poured him a glass of white wine into a fancy, tinted goblet, so its color matched my water—he's going to realize I've given up alcohol soon. Then I wore my baggiest pants and sweatshirt to bed to hide my changing body. I sweated through the sheets and mattress pad; perspiration gathered in every fold of my skin. Blake kept setting the back of his hand against my forehead to see if I had a fever. In the morning, he suggested I phone the doctor.

When he said goodbye, he stood dejected at the front door for a while before saying he enjoyed dinner and thanking me, but something was different. Stuffiness lingered in the air around us. A formalness never present before.

The words of that woman in the bathroom resounded in my head.

Bill says there's a rumor he had a mistress all along.

On Tuesday evening, Blake and I and Evy and Bennett play bocce under the lights at nearby courts until nearly eleven. He doesn't ask to stay because my kids are home.

When he drops me off, we share a quick Coke in the kitchen, and he asks if we can go to dinner alone on Thursday. I check my kitchen calendar. I've got a board meeting. Blake peeks over my shoulder. My week is full, and Blake is out of town this weekend, taking his girls to an Ohio amusement park.

"No, I can't, but we're meeting Evy and Bennett on Friday for dinner. That little bayfront restaurant."

"I want to go alone." The seriousness in his voice heightens, and worry pings across me.

"Okay," I respond. He sets down his Coke and heads toward the front door without saying more. I glance back at my calendar, confused. He sounds mad. I follow him, stammering, "I'll call Evy and let him know we aren't going."

He nods. "Okay. I'll pick you up at five-thirty."

His mood has changed. Where usually we chat for an hour saying goodnight, tonight he's ready to dash out the door.

What went wrong? Am I being too quiet?

He offers no kiss, no hug, nothing. When he stops and turns, I think he'll reach for me. Show some affection. But instead, he asks me a question—about golf.

"How was last week's classic?"

I'm so perplexed over how he's acting and so tired of talking about golf, but I put my best-girlfriend foot forward and respond. "Very good. We raised a lot of money."

"John Everglade mentioned he saw you."

Ugh. John Everglade and his wife are catty philanthropists who dangle money above everyone's head. I had successfully avoided them throughout the entire event only to catch them staring at me as I drove away with Lawrence. Janice hates me. She's mad because Evy and I directed last year's LBGT parade to run past her house on the day of her annual garden party when she entertains her stuffy, highfalutin friends.

Janice once referred to her family as "The Kennedys of Fairview." She tucks her chubby little fingers into the back pocket of any politician she can come within five feet of. I was in a book club with her for a while. Had to listen to her preach marriage is between a man and a woman. Evy and Bennett can't stand her.

"Wait." This reminds me. Blake spoke at a Town Council meeting last year and convinced the supervisors to allow that parade. He is a loyal brother to Bennett. Fully supports him. He ended up being the LBGT community's savior. "The Everglades still talk to you?"

"Not Janice. John golfs in a men's league at my club. I play a few rounds with him and his friends. We tolerate each other. He mentioned he saw you leaving with someone."

"Oh, yeah. Just Lawrence."

"The guy from work?"

"Yes, you've met him."

"No, I haven't."

"I thought you did. He's a nice guy. Smart. Quiet. But Saturday he drank too much. I drove him home."

"You didn't ride together?"

"No, he worked the early shift, and I worked later. He stayed for drinks. He and his wife are having marital problems."

An idea strikes me so hard and fast, I'm lightheaded. I should mention the nice comments Lawrence made about me. I don't brag by nature, but I have to work every angle, so Blake will see I'm marriage-worthy.

"Lawrence and I get along wonderfully. He'll be my assistant if I accept the CFO position." I haven't discussed my promotion much with Blake, because I can't take his advice seriously when he doesn't know about the pregnancy, but I'll discuss it now. Admitting my co-workers like me proves I'm at least friend-worthy. "He's thrilled I'll be his boss. Jack Bruno said I bring out the best in him."

Blake doesn't respond. I hope he's considering my cordiality.

I continue flaunting my Miss Congeniality qualities. "We've worked on several projects this past month, and I'm helping him with his communication skills. Jack said I've done a great job. Lawrence is coming out of his shell."

Blake still hasn't spoken, and I worry I'm hamming myself up too much, so I say, "But this isn't one-sided. Lawrence has helped me, too. He has a way of making me feel better about myself. He's sweet. Even defended me when Agnese started—"

"Rosy's aunt?"

"Yes, she hates me. Lawrence spoke up and defended me. Said the people at the office liked me more than her. Then he went on about how nice I was even after we left Agnese and were alone in the car."

I see Blake's mind turning, but the love and adoration I usually see in him are gone; not an ounce of affection lingers behind his cold stare. What have I said or done?

I've bungled my quiet-is-gold plan.

My desperation trips an idea. I continue, "Larry said the funniest thing on the way home."

I don't know why I'm calling him Larry, maybe so Blake thinks we are friendlier than we are. I give a little giggle and attempt to sound embarrassed by what I'm about to reveal. "He called me an angel and asked me if I would marry him. Isn't that hilarious?"

Just tossing the proposal topic to him gives me a thrill. I cross my fingers and hope this inspires him to think about a proposal himself.

"Isn't he—married?"

"Oh, yeah, his wife Lena is great. They'll be fine. I have a plan to help put a little excitement back into their marriage."

Blake's face sags. Too much bragging? I backpedal. "It's only a hitch in the road. Lena will come to her senses and see what a wonderful person Lawrence is. She's lucky to have him."

Still, not a word crosses his lips. Why is he so quiet?

I smile, flutter my eyelashes, and kiss him, but he doesn't hint about proposing or changing my last name or say anything. He leaves without another word.

Forlornly, I retire to bed, concerned that my plan isn't working. I try to reevaluate it, but this pregnancy makes me so tired I fall asleep and only vaguely hear Gianna come into my room and ask me something regarding Friday and her summer acting camp. In the morning, I forget to ask about it because she's hot on another subject.

"Where's my script?" she screams. A horn is blowing outside. Her ride is here, but it took me five attempts to get her out of bed this morning, so now she's late and in panic mode.

No one in this entire house pays me any mind until they need something.

"On the desk beside the front door." I hand her a brown bag. "Here's lunch."

She and her mustard sandwich—Gianna has a food aversion to anything without mustard—hurry away. She's off to her one-day-a-week, expensive summer acting camp, which at seven o'clock in the morning, I must remind her she begged to attend.

I listen for a thank you. Nothing. "Have a nice day," I offer, but there's no goodbye, cheerio, ta-ta. Just a grab and run.

Seems everyone's learned quiet is gold.

Chapter Thirteen - The clip

The worst thing in the world happens.

Rutger Rosy and Sugar Daddy Dave, her golf-pro main squeeze, break up. That's not bad in itself, but now she's out of the corral, blinders tightened, galloping full speed toward Blake, and after his cold departure Tuesday night, I'm worried.

To add to my dismay, after a vacation trip with her sister, Agnese returned to work on Wednesday, goading me about Rosy and encouraging me to re-watch the weekend clips of Blake's tournament. I do and I become so upset, Val, Evy, and Bennett stop by my house on Thursday after work but before my board meeting to calm me down. I replay what I've found, freezing it in the middle of a frame.

"Clearly, he has no idea she's hanging onto him." Bennett kneels on the floor and points to Blake, who's standing in a crowd, leaning to shake someone's hand. Rosy is behind him, her fingers resting on his arm.

I wonder if that's the reason he was so quiet the other night. *Has he fallen for Rosy?*

"He's right, darling. Blake is clueless. Oblivious as a turkey on a slaughter slab," Evy adds.

The advantage of dating a golf pro is the press keeps tabs on him when you aren't around. Unfortunately, so does everyone else.

"How'd you spot this?" Val asks.

"Agnese, of course. How else? I replayed Sunday's clip when I got home from work yesterday, and there it was."

"Ancient Aggie?" Evy thinks Aggie's caught in a time warp. Her hair, clothes, bobby-pinned curls beneath her ears yell 1940. "I can hardly wait to hear what she had to say."

"She said—" I speak in a high-pitched, pompous tone. I do a mean Aggie impersonation. "'Nikki, you didn't tell me you and Blake broke up.' She practically fell flat on her face rushing to tell me. I'm surprised she didn't cut her vacation short and come back Monday to rub it in."

Bennett rises from the floor. "I hope you told her to mind her own business."

"I said, 'first of all, Agnese, we didn't break up. Second, I only give you information I want the entire world to know.' She had caught me at the height of my morning nausea."

"Perfect," Evy remarks. "You're always a bear when you're sick."

"I am. I admit it."

"What did she say?"

"She explained Rosy had called her mother—that's Agnese's sister—and told her David and Rosy had broken their engagement, and Rosy was falling for someone else. Agnese saw her with Blake on the news, so blah, blah, blah, she assumed they were dating."

"I hope you bludgeoned that rumor to death with your three-inch heels."

"Loafers. I can't run to the bathroom in time to throw up in high heels."

"Loafers?" Evy's more appalled over the loafers than the story. "If you want to compete with Rutger Rosy, you can't be spotted in loafers."

"Don't worry about Rosy, Nik." Bennett squelches Evy's loafer rebuke. "The guys call her the drag-em-and-drop-em groupie. Both of the golfers she dated dropped in their standings—dramatically—as soon as they became involved with her. I'm glad you said something."

"It made me so sick I hurried to the bathroom. Of course, she followed me in, a smug smirk on her, then disingenuously apologized for striking a nerve. I told her to leave me alone. I was sick, and she says, 'There's something I've noticed about you, Nikki.' So I say, 'And I'm sure you'll tell me what that is.'

"Then I ripped a brown hand towel out of a dispenser, dabbed water on it, and patted my face, while she says, 'Every time something goes wrong around here, you conveniently say you're sick and run to the bathroom.'

"Right then, I become so sick I can't see straight. I take a step toward the stall, and she hollers, 'You're faking it.'"

"That bitch. I've only met her once," Val interjects. "Didn't like her. What'd you say?"

"Nothing. I turned around and threw up on her shoes."

Val and Evy raise their drinks and clang glasses.

For the next thirty minutes, Bennett reassures me Blake cares for me, Val disparages Aggie, and Evy fingers through magazines, flashing ugly pictures in my face of women wearing low-heeled shoes. When they leave, I hurry to my board meeting, soldier through, then return home later, sulking.

On Friday morning, I'm thankful when Blake calls to confirm our dinner. Then, twenty minutes before he picks me up, Gianna comes down the stairs carrying her overnight bag and reminds me I have to drive her to her weekend acting workshop camp in Grove City, which is an hour away.

"What do you mean I have to drive you? I thought Ellie was taking you and Olivia."

"I asked you the other night if you could switch and take us. Ellie said she'll pick us up Sunday night when it's over."

Olivia and Gianna grew up together, although since Olivia began playing soccer, they see less of each other. This makes them more excited when their paths do cross.

"Can't Ellie take the two of you tonight, and I'll pick you up on Sunday?"

"No, Mom. She has plans. You said you'd switch."

"I was half asleep."

"You're always half asleep. You're lazy."

"What did you say?"

"I said you're lazy. What's wrong with you, anyway? You spend half of your life in bed."

We shimmy into a wallop of a mother-daughter fight that lasts all the way to Grove City. I call Blake on the way, and he says we will still have time for dinner. His girls are arriving later than expected. But when I arrive at the camp, I find they've scheduled a mandatory parents' meet and greet.

I call Blake and give him the bad news; I won't be back in time for dinner. He says we'll talk after he and his girls return from their amusement-park excursion.

We'll talk. Where have I heard that before? Oh, right, the doctor. When she dropped the bomb.

Before I can remind him of our golf plans with Evy and Bennett next week, he hangs up so abruptly that I sit with my cell stuck to my ear for a full minute.

When I arrive home that night, I re-watch the golf clip from last week's tournament to see if Evy's right. Despite my insecurity, it does appear Blake has no idea Rosy's grabbed his arm.

Still, my confidence plummets and I slip into bed feeling like a pregnant teenage girl whose boyfriend is breaking up with her.

Furgy and I spend half the night tossing and turning.

Chapter Fourteen - The outfit

Well, this is embarrassing.

It's Saturday and Lena and I sit, sipping pop. I feast on dry, crunchy fries, and Lena sniffles a cry in between nibbles of a roll. She thinks Lawrence is cheating on her.

"With who?" I had no qualms about helping Lena pick out clothes but wasn't up for an outing-turned-counseling session. I glance around the food court in search of a diversion.

"Someone at work."

That catapults me into consult mode.

"He can't be. I'd know."

"He gets gussied up every morning. Puts on aftershave."

I know. Everyone knows. The moment he steps into the building people know.

"Combs his hair."

Do you have to comb Larry hair?

"Before, he'd simply roll out of bed and leave. I think he's seeing someone at work."

I think for a moment. I never knew Mark was cheating on me. Could I have missed the signs with Lawrence? There's a petite woman named Lisa in our office, but she's happily married with four kids. There's Sherry. Definitely, no—she'd never. Denise? Nope. Lawrence annoys her. I can't think of another woman who might be interested in him because Lisa, Sherry, Denise, and I are the only women remotely close to Lawrence's age. The rest of the women are young. Except for—Agnese.

I shiver at the picture materializing in my head: Agnese and Lawrence getting comfy in the lunchroom. My mind moves quickly past that frightening image.

"Could be he's excited about the new job. You know. Dressing for success." I try to comfort. Lena knows Lawrence and I are up for promotions.

"He's excited, all right, but not about a new job," she counters.

"I don't see him interested in anyone at the office," I reaffirm.

"Well—" She blows her nose, wipes, then sips her drink. She's hardly eaten any of her lunch. I gulp my Coke, waiting for her to continue. "It's not—you—is it, Nikki?"

I spit Coke on her, me, the table and floor. We both stand and toss napkins around to sop up my mess. A boy with a mop arrives, cleans around us, and when we sit down, I reach across the table and place my hand over hers. "Lena, I would never. Lawrence would never."

She gazes into my eyes and smiles. "I believe you. You really are as sweet as Larry says you are."

"Maybe I'm wrong. God knows when Mark cheated on me, I didn't see it, but I was buried in denial. I can look at Lawrence more objectively, and I don't think he's cheating. Maybe this new job will help. Sometimes the same old same old gets boring."

"Maybe you're right. We've become a bit complacent since the kids have grown. Hardly ever go out. I could plan a date night. We haven't done that in years. Do you think the pink blouse and pants I picked out will do?"

"Absolutely not." I recoil my hand. "Those are perfect for work, but let's go get you a pair of sexy jeans, snazzy boots, a blouse, and a scarf totally out of your comfort zone."

Lena giggles. "I couldn't wear those things."

"You can and you will. Leave it to me."

An hour later Lena is standing in front of a mirror in jeans, boots, and a shirt so tight every wrinkle of her bra is outlined. Her two cheeks, hovering above a low-necked shirt, are candy-apple red with embarrassment. The saleslady hands her another pair of size-four jeans to try on, and Lena asks if she can try them on in a six, or possibly an eight. The saleslady and I holler, "No," at the same time. Her waist looks paper-thin in tight jeans.

"Are you sure?" she asks me right before she heads back into the dressing room.

"Lena," I assert. "Lawrence will be drooling when he sees those jeans on you. Why are you hiding your shape?"

"I don't know. Tight clothes embarrass me."

"Not anymore they don't." I pluck a green sweater off a display close by and hand it to her. "This will draw out the color of your eyes."

"But this is a medium."

"It is?"

I take it from her, replace it, grab another, and say, "Try this one."

"This is a small."

"You better believe it is. We don't want anything hiding on date night."

She smiles and throws her arms around me. Hugs me so tightly I lose my breath. "Thank you, Nikki. Thank you so much."

She heads to the dressing room, and I meander away cheerfully. A little dread hit me when I awoke this morning and remembered I had promised to help Lena shop, but I'm glad I came. I'm having fun.

I stroll along, glancing up and down the aisles in search of more enticing outfits for Lena. Before I know it, I've strolled to the end of the women's department and I stop in my tracks, face-to-face with the enemy.

There before me stands the maternity department.

I glance over both shoulders. No one is around. I step gingerly down an aisle. Glimpse a few sweaters, shiver as I pass those stretchy, elastic-band pants. I do have to admit, the maternity clothes seem nicer, brighter. Different from the last time I was pregnant. Of course, that was a thousand years ago.

I brush a hand across the budding bulge of my stomach. It's still tiny. Between my nausea and my nerves over trying to finesse Blake into proposing, I've lost seven pounds, but I'll need clothes soon.

I sift through the dresses. With my three prior pregnancies, I lost a ton of weight in the first three months then ravenously devoured my way past my original weight and gained so much that I had twenty pounds to lose after the babies were born. I wasn't one of those lucky women who lost a ton of weight breastfeeding, either. I lugged that extra weight around for months.

I think of Blake. Wonder how he treated his wife when she was pregnant. Mark constantly badgered me to lose my baby weight.

My fingers flutter across the soft fabric and stop on the bright pink material of a dress. I pull the hanger out. It's beautiful. Plain, with a simple white lace collar. Elegant.

I hold it up and bite my lip. It's lovely, but I can't buy it in front of Lena.

I spot a salesgirl folding clothes near a cash register and ask how long she can hold it.

"Forty-eight hours."

I can sneak my way back within the next two days, so I hand her the dress, and she writes my name on a slip of paper. I step away and hear, "Hi, Nikki."

It's Sherry from work.

"A—a—hi. How are you?"

"I'm good. What are you doing in the maternity department? You're not—" she laughs a little.

I laugh back.

"Oh, yeah. Like that could happen," I say. "I'm shopping with a friend. She's pregnant and loves this dress but wouldn't buy it for herself. I'll sneak back later and buy it for her."

I put a finger to my lips. "Sh. She doesn't want anyone to know she's pregnant."

"How sweet of you."

"Oh." I wave a hand, my cheeks burning with shame.

"Is she having a girl?"

"What?"

"You picked out pink. Is she having a girl?"

"Yes. Yes. She is, as matter of fact. A girl. Don't you love baby girls?" I don't know what I'm saying. I babble on, trembling, because while normally I love being in Sherry's company, now I want to flee her fast.

We chat a while. Sherry announces she's going to be a grandmother for the first time. She's ecstatic. Chatty. I can't shake her. She's helping her daughter-in-law pick out maternity clothes and blah, blah, blah, she hopes she has a girl, too.

I shift my weight, bite my nails, pee my pants a little, and finally, her daughter-in-law shows up. Sherry introduces us, I pay no attention to what the girl's name is, and, after a minute, they promenade, arms full, toward the maternity dressing room.

I scurry back to the women's department. Lena's already back inside changing, but the saleslady assures me she's convinced her to buy the jeans, green sweater, and a more flattering bra.

After she's changed, we wander to the jewelry counter and select pieces to match each of the four outfits she's purchased. By the time we finish, I help her carry eight bags of items to the parking lot. We giggle like two schoolgirls shopping for a new year.

We are almost at our cars when it happens. Sherry spots us. I nudge Lena forward with the gentle touch of my hand to her back, but she stops.

"Isn't that Sherry from work?" She asks.

"Yeah." I toss Sherry a running-late wiggle of my fingers. "But I better be going."

Lena glances at her phone. "I thought you didn't have to be home for an hour?"

"Sherry's a little chatty," I whisper.

"Too late," Lena whispers back. "She's on her way over."

"Hi, Sherry," Lena says before I can stop her. "You may not remember me. I'm Larry's wife."

I can see from the expression on Sherry's face that, one, she doesn't recognize Lena, two, she has no idea who Larry is and, three, her gaze is focused on Lena's belly. Fortunately, Lena's wearing her normal baggy clothes.

"Larry Looney," Lena says.

Sherry's face brightens in surprise. "Ohhhh," she marvels. "Lawrence's wife."

They chat on. Sherry graciously never mentions the pregnancy. Lena sings my praise for helping her select new clothes. Right after we say our goodbyes and Lena turns toward her car, Sherry smiles at me and winks.

This little lie is not going to end well.

If I could sell my bad luck, I'd own a mansion in the Caribbean. And an island in the Pacific.

Chapter Fifteen - The lies

Work is a jungle. Its vines crisscross, and my lies multiply.

I wait for Sherry to arrive on Monday morning and ask her not to tell a soul about Lena's pregnancy. I insist I've been sworn to secrecy. Even Lawrence doesn't know. Lena wants to surprise him at a special dinner. Sherry asks when and instead of answering I don't know, I tell her in three weeks.

I have no idea why I've spewed these tales. On my way to work this morning, I had decided to tell Sherry the truth, that I was pregnant. Then, whammy, out flew the lies.

When she asks why Lena's waiting so long to tell Lawrence, I stammer and stutter and say because they have a short mini-vacation planned.

"But that's odd." Sherry's sharp. "Why wouldn't she tell him right away?"

Staggeringly, I respond with the first thought that comes to my mind. "Because of the heart murmur."

I'm nearly kicking myself before I finish the sentence.

"Lawrence has a heart murmur?"

"Yes, and Lena doesn't want to shock him."

Sherry appears skeptical. She glances down the aisle toward Lawrence's empty cubicle. He hasn't arrived yet. She squints. Her eyebrows bend toward each other in doubt. Panic shoots through me. I wave her in. Whisper. "He had a vasectomy, so she's afraid he'll have a heart attack or something."

Why do I keep talking?

"Well." Sherry becomes suddenly concerned. "Is the baby his?"

OMG.

Didn't see that coming.

"Yes, yes," I say out loud, then I trip and tangle in lie after lie, saying Lena and Lawrence hadn't had much time for each other, struggled with their marriage (okay, that's true), went to counseling, and are now ravished by love—hence, the romantic weekend away. Lena will break it to Lawrence then.

By the time Sherry returns to her cubicle she's flogged by confusion, and I'm drenched in sweat.

I make mental notes: remember the three-week lie, the counseling fib, and the ravished-by-love whopper. I've got to keep these straight.

Sherry isn't the sort to gossip, so she won't blab to anyone, but she's so shocked she spends the next few minutes rolling her chair to the edge of her cubicle, peeking across the aisle, and whispering, "I can't believe it" and "what a surprise."

When Lawrence strolls into the office, Sherry steps into the aisle and heads to the kitchen for her coffee. She leans into my cubicle and whispers, "I didn't know he had it in him."

I rush to the bathroom and vomit.

The office room where I sit and where most of the accounting work is performed is a gigantic room with a high ceiling. It's divided into cubicles separated by sound-cutting partitions that only somewhat muffle noise. We refer to this room as the accountant's cube because the room is square and houses twelve of us, six to a side.

My cubicle hugs the front corner beside a grand old hall, which expands the length of one side of the building. Left down the hall are the supervisors' offices, conference room, a kitchen with a small lunch area for employees, and stairs to the second floor where the owner has his office and reception area along with an elegant conference room for interviewing clients. Right down the first-floor hall, bathrooms separate the cube with the general reception area, so the ladies room is located wonderfully close to my little cranny of my business life. If Agnese didn't have the cubicle next to me and the biggest ears (besides the biggest mouth) in the building, I'd be able to sneak away to the bathroom any time I wanted. Unfortunately, she sticks her head out in the aisle every time she hears my heel hit the floor.

Sherry's cubicle sits directly across the aisle from mine and while I normally love sitting near her, right now I'm like a mouse wedged in a corner, caught by two cats. Agnese snoops around on one side, trying to figure out why Sherry was hunched in my office whispering this morning, and Sherry shuffles papers across the aisle, snickering.

"Hi, Nikki." Lawrence stops at my cubicle on his way back from grabbing a coffee. "Thanks for taking Lena shopping."

I cower and respond as quietly as I can. "You're welcome."

"She had fun."

I'm tempted to ask if he liked the outfits but think better of it. Agnese is surely listening. I offer a simple, "We did."

Lawrence lingers for a bit then continues down the aisle. I close my eyes and wait. As expected, Aggie creeps around our adjoining wall and asks why Lena and I went shopping.

I can't track one more lie, so I tell her to mind her own business, and she pouts all morning, banging on her computer keys, sighing, and slapping papers on her desk so forcefully that the partitions can't muffle her annoyance.

I'm the first person to hit the conference room for the staff meeting. I arrive ten minutes early because I need a few minutes of peace, but Sherry shows up less than a minute later.

She dips down as she passes me, her mouth to my ear. "Who knew Lawrence was a stud daddy?"

I reach a hand to my forehead and close my eyes.

How do I get myself into these situations?

Lawrence arrives. My cheeks burn. I've got to do something about this story I've cooked up. After the meeting, I ask Sherry to lunch, wondering if it is too soon to say Lena called and said her pregnancy test presented a false positive. But that thought is moot because, one, I remember I've told her she's far enough along to know she's having a girl, and, two, Lisa asks if she can join us. Denise would like to go, too. I spend the entire day and all week long trying to right my wrong but can't get Sherry alone.

By the end of the day on Friday, I'm wishing I was anybody but me—even Lawrence. My nausea is worse. My workload, heavier, and I'm unable to clean up the mess of lies I've concocted.

By Saturday, the Lena lie sits half-baked in the oven alongside my secret little bun. But the oven door opens and the truth comes out, appropriately, while I'm doing the one thing I hate most in life—swinging a club.

Chapter Sixteen - The ball washer

The argument begins diplomatically.

"I didn't think you wanted me to go," I say, carelessly.

Evy, Bennett, Blake, and I are golfing at a nine-hole course, and Blake and I have plenty of time to chat because a lady in a lemony blouse, a bright green skort, and a baseball cap that reads "Save the Turtles" is golfing in the foursome in front of us. She swings a minimum of five times whenever she steps up to the ball. If she knocks it less than twenty yards, she retrieves the ball, replaces it on the tee or approximately where it was on the fairway, and swings again.

While I don't mind her multiple mulligans, I do not have the patience to wait for her to meander around the fairway retrieving balls. At this rate, we won't finish until next week. We're only on the third hole.

"What did you say?" Blake asks.

I'm befuddled today and not paying attention. I only half hear him.

Turtle Lady sets her ball on the tee and swings. It rolls five feet. She retrieves the gosh-darn thing. Temporarily, I forget what Blake and I are talking about.

I've hardly slept all week and have that deer-in-the-headlights grogginess going on. I'm exhausted and it's only eleven o'clock in the morning. My concentration is lost in a fog of fatigue and fabricated stories I can no longer track. My mind is like a block of cement. It can't absorb anything.

What was I talking about?

Oh, yeah, Hilton Head.

"I thought you wanted to go alone." I'm unsteadily standing on the edge of a mediocre day that could tip either way. My nausea is mild. My disposition, so-so, but I'm so tired I can't think straight. Plus, I'm golfing, and this woman in the turtle hat is trying my patience.

I stare at her. She's struggling to set the ball on her tee.

For a moment, I forget who I'm talking to. I forget everything. "I thought you were letting me down easy."

"About the weekend?"

Turtle Lady swings again and this time she misses the ball completely, but the breeze of her swing pushes the ball off the tee, and it rolls a few inches.

"No, about everything."

"What do you mean everything? As in—our relationship?"

This woman is maddening. She replaces her ball painstakingly slowly. Now she's playing with her gloves.

"Yeah." I'm so worn-out and exasperated that I'm not paying attention to anything I'm saying. "The relationship."

Our light conversation comes to a screeching halt.

Wait. What did I say?

I glance toward my fellow golf partners. Evy's eyes are shut. Bennett stares at the ground. Blake's mouth is agape. I've admitted the truth. To Blake. I've let the fear I've been harboring for weeks escape.

"You thought, concerning our relationship, I was letting—" Blake emphasizes the next word. "You—down easy?"

"Well. Um. Yes?" I respond apologetically, remorsefully, mortified that I've loosened the latch of the elephant's cage.

"I think you're confused," he snaps.

"What?"

"I'm pretty sure it was you trying to let me down easy," he sneers, a sarcastic little hitch to his tone.

He's right. I am confused. I glance away and my nausea somersaults to the forefront. My eyes lock onto Turtle Lady. She finishes monkeying with her gloves then strolls to her bag. Replaces a club. Inspects her others.

"Wait, what?" I ask.

"You were the one, Nikki. You were letting me down easy."

Distraction. Inattentiveness. These must be Nikki defense mechanisms because I can't seem to stay focused on my conversation with Blake.

He's never been irritated with me. This is a first. Unfortunately, I do what I always do when I feel threatened. I snap. "I wasn't the one breaking up. You were."

"What?"

Have I gone too far?

I'm so weary I don't know.

"Breaking up? We're breaking up?" He repeats, leans away. "I certainly wasn't breaking up with you."

My gaze wanders over to the Turtle Lady while my mind searches for some recovery ploy. The woman keeps withdrawing clubs then setting them back in her bag, and I keep searching.

"I—I—"

The lady can't decide which club to use. I feel the blood rise to my cheeks.

"I was—you were—I mean—" Does Turtle Lady not care seven people are waiting for her to swing? Who does that? Who can function in their own little world and shut everything and everybody out so easily?

"I—I wasn't the one cheating."

Did I say cheating? I meant to think that.

"Cheating?" Blake says this so loud he doesn't just grab my attention, he grabs everyone's attention.

Evy mumbles, "Oh, joy, here we go."

"It was you." The veins on Blake's neck bulge. "I wasn't cheating. You were."

He's finally caught my undivided attention.

"Me?" I blurt out.

"Yeah, you. You were the one cheating. Not me." He shoves his golf club back into his bag as if he's about to leave.

"Me?" I repeat.

"Yeah. You."

"Oh, no, no, no, no. You're not blaming this on me. You were the one cheating. You had another woman perched on your arm in Hilton Head."

Turtle Lady hears me and stops searching for a club. She shoots me a gaze. I wave a finger at her. "Just pick a club and swing," I shout.

"I get one mulligan," she has the nerve to croak.

"One—that's the keyword here," I holler.

Blake steps between her and me to capture my attention.

"As in one woman." I poke him in the chest. "As in you should date one woman at a time."

"I was only dating one woman."

"Oh, really?"

"Really."

"Well, that's a lie. Ask Evy and Bennett." I point to them. "We saw the clip of you and Rutger Rosy standing together."

I see the fear in both Evy and Bennett. Their eyes widen.

"You think I'm dating Rutger Rosy?"

"It was on TV, Blake, go back and look for yourself. Tell him, Evy. Bennett."

They say nothing.

"You weasels. Go hide in the chicken coop where you belong."

Both of them step away.

"I am not dating Rosy." He inserts a nasty little chuckle between words, and for the first time in fourteen months, I become enraged with him.

"How do I know what you do at these tournaments? And don't you dare laugh at me. That's what Mark always did."

"I'm not Mark, and I don't cheat."

"Boy, doesn't that sound familiar." My eyes search my surroundings. I've golfed on this course before. I know there's a ball washer somewhere at this tee. I need to smash something. "I wish I had a dollar for every guy who said he doesn't cheat."

When I golfed with Mark, I took my frustration out on my balls. I knew the location of every ball washer on every golf course, and there's one here, somewhere on the third hole, but I'm so mad I can't locate it. I turn back toward Blake. Stab a finger at his chest, again. "People say you golfers have women at every golf course."

"Women?"

"Yeah, women."

"At every golf course?"

"Yep." I fold my arms. "That's what they say."

He steps away and crosses his arms. "Say it."

"Say what?"

"Say, with a straight face, that you think I'm having a fling with Rutger Rosy."

"A fling?" This word infuriates me. I fix my hands on my hips.

"Yeah, a fling." He sets his hands on his hips, imitating me.

"Funny you should mention fling. That's what people said about you and me. They said I was your fling." I wave one hand dramatically in the air.

"You are not a fling."

"Well, I feel like a fling. I'm a fling. Rosy's a fling. How many flings do you have?"

"You honest to God think I'm having a fling with Rutger Rosy?"

I don't suppose he'd be referring to her as Rutger Rosy if he was sleeping with her, but I'm too far into this argument to back down now.

"Why not? She's beautiful. Shallow. Her manicured fingers—on your arm!—reflect perfectly in the light of the camera, and her stupidity makes you look like Einstein. Isn't that what you want? A dumb girl to pump up your ego?"

"Oh, so I want a dumb girl?"

"Yeah, you do." I'm unintelligibly arguing, but I'm so mad there's no time to stop and regroup.

"Okay, who are you making look like Einstein?"

"Excuse me? Are you insinuating I'm stupid?"

"No, I'm insinuating that it's you who's having the fling."

"What is that supposed to mean?"

A man on a golf cart riding by slows, catching my attention, and I realize the entire foursome in front of us is listening. Turtle Lady is standing by her bag. Her ball is still perched on its tee.

I take twenty steps toward her ball. I'm like Adam Sandler in that golf movie, which Mark made me watch umpteen hundred times. Evy asks what I'm doing as I dart toward Turtle Lady's ball and swing with the might of God, sending her golf ball two hundred feet smack dab down the middle of the fairway.

"Well, I never—" she begins saying.

"Go get your ball," I scream and point.

She and her little friends scurry toward their golf carts.

"You're going to get us banned from this course, Naggy."

I ignore Evy because, at long last, I've located the ball washer. I stomp toward it and take my frustration out on my ball, pumping it up and down so hard the machine froths.

Blake ignores Evy, too. "When I was in Hilton Head, you left the charity classic with another guy."

"Sure, make things up." I pump harder.

"I'm not making anything up. You admitted it. And if you break that, you're paying for it."

I look him straight in the eye and pump harder. We both hear something crack. I keep pumping.

"I'm not paying for any more of your tantrums."

"Well, excuse me. I tend to have tantrums when the guy I'm dating is cheating on me."

"Really? Me? Why don't you tell me about Larry?"

"Who?"

"Larry. From work. You went home with him that Saturday I was in Hilton Head."

"Let me get this straight." I stop pumping. "You think I'm cheating on you with Larry-haired Lawrence?"

He shakes his head. Squints. "Larry hair?"

"Larry David hair. What woman cheats with a man who has Larry David hair?"

"Androgenetic alopecia," Evy slips in.

"Apparently, you," Blake says.

"I would never cheat on you. You cheated on me." I tug at the top of the ball washer. It's broken. I toss it on the ground.

"Just tell him, Nikki," Evy shouts.

"Yeah, tell me. The truth. Are you sleeping with Larry?"

"What?" I nearly choke on my tongue.

"You were all goo-goo-eyed over him the other day. Said he was sweet, smart, having marital problems."

"That's not what I—"

"You were helping him out. Remember? Putting a little bit of the magic back in his marriage."

"Did you really say that?" Evy butts in.

"No; that's not what I said."

"Just tell me the truth. Do you like him?"

"Are you crazy? Have you seen him?" This comes out cold-heartedly. There isn't anything wrong with the way Lawrence looks. I mentally apologize. He's not bad looking, just not for me. "You want to know if I like Lawrence-not-Larry?"

"Yes."

"You've never met Lawrence or you wouldn't ask. Trust me. I have no feelings for him."

Evy vouches for me. "I can back her on this one. She definitely doesn't like Larry."

"Gee, thanks for crawling out of the coop," I holler at him. He steps behind Bennett.

"Well, something's wrong. You don't talk anymore," Blake shouts. "I can barely coax a sentence out of you."

"I was trying to make you think I was smart."

"What?"

"I was pretending I was smart. I was cooking for you. Cleaning for you. Doing everything a nice little girlfriend should do."

"Exactly. One day you were wonderful, too good to me, and the next day you wanted nothing to do with me. You hardly spoke to me. Every time I touched you, you flinched."

"So this is about sex?"

"TMI, kids," Evy shouts over Bennett's shoulder.

"This isn't about sex," Blake hollers. "It's never been about sex. I love you. But I need to know. Do you love me or not?"

"Nikki." Bennett steps forward. "Tell him."

"Tell me what?" Blake yells. "About Larry? Are you in love with Larry?"

"I don't love Lawrence."

"Well, not only do I not love Rosy, I don't even like her."

"Then why haven't you called me all week like you usually do?"

"Because your calendar said Lawrence's wife was out of town last Saturday."

"What?"

"Your kitchen calendar. You shouldn't make notes about your flings if you don't want your boyfriends to see them."

I have to think. Lena never went out of town. "What are you talking about?"

Blake has picked up his golf bag, but he slams it back onto the ground. "When you checked your calendar Monday night? I saw Saturday's note."

"What note?"

"Larry's wife. Out of town."

"Oh, my God." I slap a hand onto my forehead.

"I see you remember."

"You were out of town, Blake. You took your girls to an amusement park. The out of town was about you. Take a drive to my house and see for yourself. Every Saturday, I mark out of town or in town—for you."

"Nice try. Right below the out of town it said Lawrence's wife."

"Because I took her shopping," I scream.

"That's true," Evy acknowledges. "She did."

"Then what's wrong, Nikki? Because, clearly, you've been acting differently. Avoiding me. Not talking. If you're not having a fling with this Lawrence guy, then what are you doing?"

I can't take it anymore. I'm sick and tired. Exhausted from lying. So I shriek, "I was trying to get you to propose."

There is a moment when no one says a word. The people in the crowd that has gathered hold their breath.

"Propose?" Blake echoes, confused.

My bewilderment bursts and I break into a full-hearted cry. Bennett hustles toward me, steadying me with his hand.

"Tell him the truth," he encourages.

"What's the truth?"

Suddenly, Evy is beside me. He sets his palm against my back and rubs endearingly. "Tell him." He kisses my temple. "It will be okay. Tell him, Nik."

"Tell me what?" Blake inches toward me.

I'm crying full out. No tissue. I lift my blouse and use it to wipe snot and tears away. "My boobs were getting too big."

"Not exactly how I would have phrased it," Evy mumbles, "but go ahead."

I continue bawling, blubbering. "I wanted you to ask me to marry you before you noticed—before—"

"Before what?" Blake is so frustrated he yells the question.

"Before you found out I was pregnant."

The shapes and forms and bright colors of the day blur together behind my tears. I sob. Blow my nose. Evy's arms encircle me.

"Excuse me?" I think I hear Blake say.

I hide my face against Evy's shoulder. I can't speak. Bennett intercedes. "She's pregnant, Blake. She was afraid to tell you."

Blake approaches. "You can't—I mean. I didn't think—" He glances toward my stomach. He stands, saying nothing, waiting for me to compose myself.

"I didn't think I could either," I cry.

"You mean…you're…you're sure?"

I nod.

"You're pregnant?"

"Two and a half months." I cover my face. "Maybe three."

"Is that why you're throwing up?"

I slide my hands away from my face, gather them under my chin, and nod.

"Why didn't you tell me?"

"Because I didn't want you to propose to me because I was pregnant. I wanted you to propose because you loved me and wanted to marry me."

He stands quiet for a moment. Motionless. Then he lunges toward me, sets a hand on the back of my head, and pulls me forward, kissing me, long and hard. When his lips leave mine, he moves closer, encircles me with his arms, and says, "I love you, Nikki. There isn't a single, tiny thing I don't love about you."

"I love you, Blake, but I don't want to force you into marriage."

"Let me show you something."

He steps away, reaches into his golf bag, and pulls a small black box out of a pocket.

"I've been carrying this around for two months, trying to build enough courage to ask you. I told myself as soon as I got home from my last tournament, I'd ask you because I never wanted to win again without you at my side to help me celebrate. So I took you to dinner but everyone kept asking for autographs, and you were sick—wait."

He stops as if enlightened. "You were sick because of the pregnancy?"

I nod. He kisses my forehead.

"Then I had everything set up to ask you while we were at Hilton Head, but you wouldn't go."

"I was afraid you'd see—" I sniff and glance toward my chest.

"Nikki, you should have told me."

"I couldn't."

He steps away. "This isn't how I planned it."

I gaze into his eyes and there it is. That twinkle. That sparkle that I love. I see his cute little smirk grow, edging out the corner of his lips, his dimple peeking past a cheek, and suddenly I don't care about anything. The pregnancy. Getting married. Nothing. Only Blake.

"I wanted everything to be perfect. The place. The time. It shouldn't have mattered to me." He tugs on a pant leg, gets down on one knee, and snaps open the box.

"Marry me, Nikki. Not because of a baby. Because you love me."

I'm gazing at a diamond ring, speechless. Around us, there are no longer two foursomes. People have crawled out of the woods and gathered. Everyone holds their breath while I come to terms with what's happened. That Blake knows I'm pregnant. That he isn't proposing because I'm carrying his baby. That he's proposing because he loves me.

I gaze down at him.

"Marry me and you'll make me the happiest man alive."

"Oh, for God's sake," Evy chirps. "Say yes. Get it over with. Welcome to the family."

"Yes," I say.

Blake stands and by the time his lips reach mine, cheers rise around our suddenly crowded corner of the golf course. People shout. Phones click. There is a flash from a camera. I drink the moment in. Blake's lips are pressed against mine and his ring is around my finger. He loves me—faults and all.

For the first time in many years, I feel like I'm enough. I want this confident sensation never to end.

"By the way." His gorgeous little dimple resurfaces when I open my eyes. "Your timing might have been off, but that was one hell of a drive."

"I could sort of say the same for you." I stand on my tippy toes and find his smiling lips.

Chapter Seventeen - The kids

The rush to gather our children together is on.

While Blake's whipping out a diamond and proposing on bended knee after I tactlessly broadcast I was pregnant seemed fairytale romantic, in the aftermath we realized we should have told our kids first. After we left the golf course, we danced a jig down at the local newspaper, promising them an exclusive story on our engagement and baby if they kept it out of the paper for two days.

On the ride home, Blake called his ex and told her we were getting married, it would be in the news, and he wanted to pick the girls up first thing in the morning to bring them to Erie to tell them.

I listened to half of the conversation from the passenger seat, gathering bits and pieces of a typical discussion between two people, who never got along, trying to get along.

"Because we're telling all five of them together…yes, it is important enough for me to come get them…maybe not to you, but this is a big deal to us…" Blake carefully tiptoes around the pregnancy because if Margie finds I'm pregnant, he's afraid she'll retaliate and not let them come.

This is not an unreasonable fear. I've been in Margie's company three times while accompanying Blake to pick up his girls in Wheeling. What I remember of those encounters is her breathtaking beauty—and her cutting tongue. Granted, she has been better since she began dating her new boyfriend, Ben, but Blake's afraid she'll regress if she finds out I'm pregnant.

It's an ex thing.

"Listen," he tells her. "You can make an exception this one time. I've never asked for them other than at my scheduled times."

He gazes at me and sighs.

"Gee, thanks for the advice, but no…I'll be there at ten…no…yes…I understand."

I use this same expression when I talk to Mark, but can divorced people understand each other? Face it. If they did, they probably wouldn't be divorced. Moreover, now they've been thrust into a single world and forced to meander through life, facing once-shared problems—alone. So what are the chances they understand one another now?

There is so much to say and do and plan and think about when you're divorced: family, romance, work, health, well-being. Add stacks of problems from two or three kids and people find themselves boxed into a corner. They can't comprehend anything outside their demanding, cramped, overwhelming world.

Hence the reason "I understand" is usually followed by a "but."

"But," Blake offers, his voice straining. "I don't want them to hear this on the news."

He's quiet then suddenly snaps his neck to the right and left, glimpsing out both car windows. He swerves into a parking space and shoves the car into park.

"I am not telling them over the phone. Do not make this difficult. I'm not going to argue."

This is another glitch in divorcee lingo that I also use. Why, in the middle of an argument, do I say I'm not going to argue when I'm already arguing?

"Yes, Nikki's here with me." He reaches across the front seat and takes my hand in his. "No, I'm not telling her that."

"What?" I pantomime.

Blake shakes his head, rolls his eyes as if she's being petty.

"You have no right to pass judgment on anyone," he raises his voice.

Other than a few minutes at the golf course today, this is the maddest I've seen him—ever.

"You don't need to know…it's been two years, Margie…we are not starting this over again."

Margie forever brings up the past. The divorce. Blake's leaving. It often slips her mind that she cheated on him, and while normally I empathize with a comrade divorcee, I have zero pity for cheaters.

Blake shifts his weight in his seat. "Okay, noon, then. Goodbye."

He sets his cell back in its holder, releases my hand, and shifts into drive. I cover my face. If this is how news of our getting married goes, I can't imagine what Margie will say when she finds out I'm pregnant. Or, dear Lord, what Mark's reaction will be.

"I'm so sorry," I whisper.

"For what?"

"Everything. Being pregnant. Divorced. If I was younger, I'd—" I hesitate.

He shifts back into park.

"You'd what?" His tone has softened. "Be happy?"

"I'm not sure. Be excited?"

"I hope this isn't my fault. That I've made you sorry you're pregnant." He reaches for my hands, gathers them into his. "When the gravity of everything hit me, I was shocked. But for a split second when you first told me, when I wasn't thinking of my age or our kids or that we weren't married. At that moment, you know what I felt?"

"What?"

"Pure joy."

"You did?"

"I did. I looked into your eyes and this euphoric surge somewhere deep inside me rose up and took my breath away."

"I love you, Blake." I snap a tissue from a box on the floor of his car and dab my eyes.

"Listen." He pulls me close. "We're in this together."

He's so sweet, and I'm so lucky to have his support. I don't know why I'm crying. "I hope you know that if I'd had any suspicion I could have gotten pregnant, I would have gone on the pill."

"Didn't you ever wonder about it, though?"

"About what?"

"What our kids would be like?" He tightens his grip on me. "Because I have. Once or twice, I wondered what type of parents we would have been together. What our child would be like. Now I'll find out. So—" He kisses me again. "Don't be sorry. I'm not."

His gaze sweeps across my face. He lifts a hand and strokes my hair, tenderly. "Never in my wildest dreams did I imagine I'd find someone like you. I've been in love with you since the day I first spotted your pouty little face in the back of the crowd at that golf lesson. I even love that you hate golf."

"I don't hate golf."

"Yes, you do." He smiles then kisses me gently, his lips grazing mine, softly, lightly, as if I'm so fragile I might crumble. Tears trickle down my face. He wipes them away with the thumb of one hand. "You go on and let that pretty head of yours worry about this baby, the kids, life, and everything else, but you never worry about this one thing: I love you, Nikki Stone. I always will."

He stretches his reassuring arms around me, there, on the side of the road, in the dim light of a streetlamp, the car running and the moon peeking down on us. His warm embrace is exactly what I need in this messy moment. We drive to my house, and for once we put ourselves and our relationship first, before everyone else, and he spends the night. We make love, quietly, because my kids are home. For some reason, nothing matters anymore.

In the morning, the kids don't bat an eye when they see him at the kitchen table, drinking coffee. He leaves to spend a few hours working at the club, then takes off for Wheeling to pick up his girls. I work most of the day, leave an hour early, and we meet back at my house around five o'clock.

Everyone is waiting and accounted for by quarter after the hour, except Delanie, who's on her way.

I bring out a pitcher of lemonade, and Blake sets three pizzas on the table. The kids devour the food, and we head to the family room for what Blake announces is "a talk."

"It's not like we can't see the ring on Nikki's finger, Dad. I don't know why you have to make a production of this." Sophie plops next to Gianna on the love seat and crosses her arms.

Blake has two daughters. Sophie, the spitfire, is eight months younger than Gianna, and Hannah, the gentle spirit, is eighteen months Gianna's senior. Sophie and Gianna have struck a friendship in the past year from which Hannah is often removed.

Though she's the older of the three, Hannah is sweeter and kinder, which dashes my "first children scare me" philosophy. Hannah also measures three inches shorter than Gianna and Sophie, whose long, lean legs seem tangled together when they walk down the street telling secrets. Fortunately, on the days our two families spend together, Hux tugs Hannah into the mix with a little tender-loving teasing, remedying all. He doles out attention to Hannah at the first sign of her being left out, and Sophie, who has a crush on Hux, suddenly forgets the qualities she doesn't like in her sister.

"A few more minutes won't kill you, Sophie. Delanie will be home soon." Blake sets his glass of water on the coffee table. He has several coasters to choose from, with quips such as "our home," "show kindness," or "strong soul," but subconsciously, and appropriately, he selects the one marked "be brave."

He sits and I settle next to him on the couch just about the time Delanie arrives, grabs the piece of pizza I've hidden away for her, and joins us in the family room. I scoot backward, nudging against the back cushions, so I am as far away from the kids as I can get. I fix my gaze on my lap. Blake, always the optimist, is perched on the edge of his seat with unwavering, oblivious hope. He stretches a hand toward mine, and we interlock fingers.

Hux sees our clasped hands. "Is someone dying or something?"

"No, actually, we have good news." Blake shoots a smile toward me. I return a minuscule grin. "Nikki and I are getting married."

Sophie snorts a laugh.

"No kidding," Gianna barks.

"Duh, yeah," Hux says.

Blake clears his throat. "We have some even better news," he ventures. Then he makes the terrible mistake of nervously glancing toward me, and in that tenth of a second, Delanie shoots straight up like a firecracker.

"You have got to be kidding," she explodes.

I cover my eyes with my free hand.

"What?" Gianna jumps up beside her sister, facing her. "What's wrong?"

"She's—" Delanie begins answering, stops, and tosses a chastising look my way. "Is that why you're…" Her gaze darts to my chest then back to my eyes. "Please tell me you're not—"

She can't say it. She glares at me, the heat of her stare blazing across the room, scorching me. She hesitates for one brief calm-before-the-storm second, and everyone in the room holds their breath.

Then the hurricane hits.

"You're pregnant?" Gianna shrieks.

"Are you out of your mind?" Delanie takes several steps to the right, then the left, as if she wants to run but has nowhere to go. Her feet slip back into the exact spot where she began.

"Oh, my God." Hux's voice is ten pitches higher than I've ever heard it. "You're—"

"Going to have a baby?" Hannah finishes for him, then a long moment of quiet strikes the room.

Foolishly, I wonder if this might not be as bad as expected, but eventually Sophie stands and crushes my hope. She utters three simple words that make me want to fold inside myself.

"You. Had. Sex?"

"Sex?" Gianna repeats the one word that has always been hard for me to say in front of my children, and like Delanie, I want to run, too.

"Now, girls." Clearly, Blake doesn't understand a teenage girl's temperament because he attempts to calm the room with reasoning. "When two people love each other—"

"Blake," I interrupt, tugging his arm, hoping to thwart any birds-and-bees tutorial.

He turns toward me and holds up a hand. "Nikki, let me handle this," he says. "Sophie, Gianna, it's called making love, and it's perfectly nat—"

"It's called screwing," Sophie says to Gianna.

"Old people don't screw," Gianna replies.

"Make love," Blake corrects.

Gianna fixes her gaze on me and though I didn't think it possible, the room gets hotter. "So you're knocked up."

My cheeks erupt, and the burning inside me spreads like a wildfire. I'm covered in shame.

"Oh, my God," Hux howls. "Mom's knocked up."

"That's not—" Blake tries to interject, but at this point, no one knows he's in the room.

"You're too old to have a baby," Gianna says.

"Too old to have sex." Sophie covers her eyes as if a mental picture has struck her.

"Love has no age, Sophie." Blake with another naive attempt at a life lesson. "When two—"

"So, like, do grandma and grandpa George do it?" Sophie's hands slide down her face.

"Oh, please, not them." Hannah's climb up hers, covering her eyes.

"Wait." Hux has an aha moment. He stops laughing. "Does this mean old people—older than you guys—do it? Unbelievable."

"Making love has no age limit, Hux," Blake responds.

"That is disgusting," Gianna says.

"Don't your ovaries dry up and fall out or something when you're old?" Sophie cringes, and the entire room breaks into a unified "Ewwww."

"What happened to all those lectures about saving yourself for marriage, Mom?" Delanie crosses her arms, and in that split second, I realize how much she's grown to look like me.

"You're not going to keep doing it, are you?" Gianna asks. "While we're in the house?"

"They don't do it here." Sophie's appalled. "Where do you do it? In a car?"

Hannah starts crying.

"Do people have sex while they're pregnant?" Gianna whispers to Sophie, and this sends Blake over the edge.

He stands and hollers. "Stop, all of you. I love Nikki and yes, we make love."

I use both hands to cover my face.

Another moment of silent shock stretches across the room, then Hux breaks into hysterics and, unitedly, the girls start screaming:

"That's repulsive."

"Embarrassing."

"I'm not changing a single diaper."

"Me either."

"Me either."

"I'm glad we live with Mom—wait—do Mom and Ben do it? Gross."

"I want to live with Dad—oh, my God, is Dad doing it?"

"Well, obviously, Gianna."

"Disgusting!"

The offensive dialogue continues for several minutes until the girls leave the room in rapid succession. Upstairs, bedroom doors slam, one by one. Hux leaves shortly after them, tears of laughter streaming down his face.

"So." Blake sits, sweat trickling down one side of his face, the back of his shirt, soaked. "That went well."

I sit in my own puddle of shame on my side of the couch then I realize it's not humiliation, it's incontinence.

Great. Just great.

I run to the bathroom, at least relieved that they haven't sent me into a full-blown seizure.

Chapter Eighteen - The appointment

I call Jack Bruno shortly after we tell our kids because I want him to know about my pregnancy before it hits the morning news. The kindness his family has shown me over the years, both before I had kids and after, has been generous. In a world where women fight for rights, the Bruno family fights for women.

This isn't a one-way street, though. I've worked hard for them, too.

I never understood supervisors, managers, and owners who treated employees poorly. Most people want to feel as if they are contributing to the good of their company. Treat them as if they are, and their loyalty compounds. Act as if they are a payroll burden, and they won't work half as hard for you.

This is so clear to me, and yet, lots of employers don't see this. Mine does.

Jack's father built his company into what it is today. He is by no means perfect, but one thing he did right was raise hard-working, compassionate kids. Neither his son nor daughter grew up in an anything-you-want world. Both worked the business from the ground up. As teenagers, they cleaned offices, emptying trash cans and sweeping floors. By the time I came on board in my younger years, Jack had graduated from college and was sitting for his CPA exam. Once he passed, his dad didn't advance him to the top. He remained a staff accountant for several years.

When his dad retired, Jack was ready.

So telling him before the news hit the paper was nearly as important to me as telling my kids. As expected, Jack takes the news stoically.

"Nikki, I'm happy for you," he remarks, his sincerity undisguisable even over the airwaves. "I have only met Blake a few times, but he seems like a wonderful person. I know—" The phone goes quiet and I wait patiently. I've always admired Jack for his candor and well-placed words. He thinks before he speaks—a trait I'd much like to acquire. "You have had a tough time in the past. I want to wish you and Blake much happiness."

I jump on his next hesitation.

"I understand this might impact my ability to carry the workload of the CFO." I could lie for the sake of women and say it won't, but all of the feminism in the world won't change the fact that I won't be getting as much sleep at night and may not be able to put in the long hours I sometimes do now.

Before I can continue, Jack cuts me off.

"I'm not rescinding my offer if that's what you're worried about. I would never. Getting married and having a baby will change things, yes, but you know what I have found?" He doesn't wait for me to answer. "Mothers are conscientious and organized. They've got something to prove, and I've seen them prove it over and over. They're—I'm not sure if this is politically correct to say, but I'm saying it, anyway. They are happier. And I have always believed: happy employees, happy employer."

Glad to have told him over the phone, I disguise my voice so he doesn't know I'm crying. A compassionate employer is a hidden gem in today's world. I'm blessed to work for the Brunos.

With that accomplished, my employer informed, I sleep soundly, and in the morning, the first person I head toward is Sherry. The news hasn't unfolded in the media. Technically, the forty-eight hours isn't up until dinner time tonight. So I seek out Sherry and explain that I hadn't told Blake or my kids yet when I ran into her at the mall. I apologize for lying and she understands.

"I would have done the same myself," she admits.

"Thank you for not telling anyone." Sherry and I have grown to trust each other completely in the past year.

"You're welcome but, Nikki? Did you say something to Agnese?"

"No, why?"

"Maybe it was my imagination because I was trying to keep what you told me about Lena secret, but Agnese has been pumping me with questions lately—about both you and Lawrence."

"What kind of questions?"

"She's been asking about your stomach problems, which I never thought anything about because you've had those issues since the day you began working here." What Sherry says is true. Even before my pregnancy, my stomach churned with the slightest of worry. "But then the other day she began pelting me with questions about Lawrence. She wanted to know if he and Lena were getting along. As if I had some inside secret."

"What did you tell her?"

"That I had no idea. It was none of my business and none of hers, either."

"Think she overheard us?"

"Maybe," Sherry drawls, her pitch alarmingly worrisome.

I roll this around all morning and decide to tell the entire office I'm pregnant at lunch. I specifically watch Agnese's expression. Her face melts from cold-hearted curiosity to heated abashment. She makes no attempt to mask her disapproval, gasping dramatically. Her mouth gapes and her eyes bulge. She can't speak, she's so caught by surprise.

The others congratulate me kindly. A few girls take me aside and ask how I'm doing. Denise is my age and she offers the best congratulations. "I'm sure you're shocked, and I know it will be difficult raising a newborn at our age, but Nikki, I think of what a better parent I would be today than I was twenty years ago, so I am happy for you. You and Blake will be fabulous parents."

Some snickers circulate among my younger coworkers. I walk into the kitchen that afternoon and hear the thirty-year-old accountant, Lawrence Peter, whom we call Peter so as not to confuse him with Lawrence-not-Larry, asking one of the girls how old a woman has to be before she can't have babies. But all in all, everyone is nice.

For the remainder of the day, I immerse myself in work. I have three critical accounts with financials due and Blake has lessons tonight, so I work well past seven. When I'm leaving, I'm surprised to find Agnese still there. She hardly ever offers to work overtime.

"Nikki," she calls, rushing toward me. "I must ask. I'm sure no one else had the nerve, but are you sure you're pregnant?"

"Yes, I am." I sigh. There's no limit to her rudeness.

"Have you seen a doctor?"

"Not that it's any of your business but, yes, I have."

"Did they do a blood test?"

"Who are you, my mother?"

"You don't have to get snotty."

"It's hard not to when snot drips from nosy people."

She sucks in an appalling breath. "I was showing concern, not being nosy."

"Yeah, right." I snort a laugh.

"There is such a thing as a false positive, you know."

"I'm going to the doctor tomorrow afternoon. Want to come?"

She stomps away mad, murmuring under her breath something about people being discourteous when you're only trying to help. So I murmur I'll ask for a doctor's excuse for nosy coworkers.

She hears me and shouts a rebuttal, "You'll be the oldest mother at the labor and delivery class."

Do they even have those classes anymore?

I don't respond because my mind races away on the labor class. I slam the door behind me, go home, and cry to Blake on the phone.

He says don't pay attention to her, she's just like Rosy, then he begs to go to my appointment, innocently, charmingly, like a little boy whining for ice cream. His sweet insistence drowns out Agnese's pessimism like the music of an ice-cream truck on a sweltering day after you've been bullied at the playground. I'm ecstatic he wants to come along, and the next day we walk into Doctor Yank's office holding hands, timid smiles curving our lips.

Doctor Yank arrives at my examining room in a merry mood. She's not rushed today. She spends fifteen minutes talking about the pros and cons of having a baby at my age, explaining my type of epilepsy medication typically has little effect on a baby, and saying she'll require additional ultrasounds and blood work, concentrating mostly on the positive. I've only seen this woman three times before today, so I don't know her well, but she's appeared formal before this appointment. Today she's chatty, kind, downright perky, the smile on her face unbending.

Then I realize she hasn't taken her eyes off Blake.

"And who knows," she titters. "Maybe this baby will be another golf pro."

Is she flirting with him in front of me?

I don't care. I'm not proud. I'll lick up any ice cream that spills over the edges of Blake's cone.

"So, Doctor," he begins—I'm not sure he knows her name because I call her Yank. "What precautions should Nikki be taking? She's pretty driven. Doesn't sit much. She's an avid runner. Is the running okay at her…stage?"

He's kindly added that "st."

"That is an exceptional question, Mr. Anderson. So glad to see a father who is concerned with the health of both mother and baby."

Give me a break.

"All indication is Nikki is in good health, especially for someone forty-seven-years-old." Doctor Yank doesn't mind mentioning my age. She's unconcerned with me altogether. Her eyes remain fixed on Blake. I'm not sure she knows I'm here.

"But I do think you're right, Blake." Formality has slipped out the edges of the door. He's her friend now. "Let's take a look at her and see how far along she is."

She hovers over me with her gadgets, taking my temperature, checking my heart and blood pressure, measuring my stomach, and in less than two minutes, she announces I'm fit and turns back to Blake.

"She's barely showing, so I'm not sure of a due date. I'll mark her as four months for now, but we will set up a sonogram to be sure."

Because I haven't had a period, I could only guess how far along I was. I had counted back to when I began getting sick and estimated three months on Doctor Yank's forms. I'm elated she's said I might be further along. A month might not sound like much, but if you're pregnant and puking, it's huge. The nausea usually lessens in the second trimester.

I count back in my head. Four months means I'm approximately sixteen weeks pregnant. That's possible. I should stop throwing up soon.

"So, how much running is safe for her at this point in time?" Blake asks.

Doctor Yank folds her arms, tucking her iPad to her chest. "She should cut back. Maybe walk instead. How many miles does she run a week?"

Hello, I'm over here.

Blake glances at me, witnessing my frown. He raises his eyebrows, and I wave my hand in a go-ahead-and-answer motion. He stifles his laugh by clearing his throat.

"Over forty miles a week. Is that about right, Nik?" He invites me to participate.

"Approximately. Three mornings during the week, a long run on Saturday, and an easy six on Sunday."

"Oh. You should cut back," Doctor Yank snaps. At long last, she's looked at me.

Blake jumps in. "You can tell her to quit running, but she won't. She has too much excess energy. How much is safe?"

She breaks her brief eye contact with me and answers him sweetly. "She ought to keep the weekly mileage to, oh, let's say fifteen or less."

"Fifteen?" My squeal bounces off Doctor Yank's backside. She's facing Blake. "So, what? Do I run them all at once?"

That catches her attention. She turns toward me, and annoyance creeps back into her tone. "No. You need to cut way down. No more than four a day. Fifteen a week."

And so begins my middle-age pregnancy.

Chapter Nineteen - The article

One day after the local news runs the article about our engagement and my pregnancy, my name in the sports world becomes as common as French fries on a fast-food menu.

For a week, I'm a celebrity. Everything is about me. National television, local news, magazines. Newscasters have Nikki Stone perched on the tip of their tongues. Okay, not in a great way, but for years I've been an unnoticed mom, nothing more. Up until now, my notability was a negative number on a scale of one to ten. Not anymore.

Now I'm the pro's pregnant forty-seven-year-old fiancée.

At home and work, age-and-pregnancy comments fly. My family showers me with attention. They notice and mention my illness, temperament, and feelings.

"Is that why you're puking?" Gianna.

"Does pregnancy make women moody?" Hux.

"This has exponentially increased your sensitivity." Delanie.

Normally, to my kids, I'm like a coat of old paint hidden by three newer, livelier overlayers—them. Now I'm a fresh, trendy color, and my new hue astonishes them. I don't compete with sit-coms and reality TV for their attention anymore. I am reality TV.

At work, it's the same. Yesterday, we acquired five new clients, all of them requesting me for their accounting services. Agnese equates this to everyone wanting to see the good-looking pro's freaky girlfriend, but I don't care. When you're a mom who's been ignored for years, in a career that's only a hair more exciting than an envelope stuffer, even bad attention spices up your dull existence.

Today, my kids and I are sharing some quality time together. Unfortunately, it's around an unbecoming picture of me in a national gossip magazine.

"This isn't exactly stardom, Mom," Delanie points out. "They're calling you SandTrap."

"As in you trapped Blake into marrying you." Gianna feels she must clarify.

Hux, on the other hand, points to the silver lining. "At least she ditched the ForePlay nickname." He leans over the table to speed read the article. "Wait. Nope. It's hanging on. 'Sources stated Nikki Stone is also known in the golf community as ForePlay Nikki for hollering "fore" in the direction of her mislaid ball and "play" in the other direction. Stone logged a thirty-seven over par at a recent Ohio charity classic.' Really, Mom? Thirty-seven over par?"

"They made me count my whiffs."

"You're supposed to count your whiffs," Gianna scolds.

"How do you know that?"

"Everyone knows that."

"Not people who hate golf. Don't I get a mannigan or something?"

"Oh, my God, a mulligan." Delanie throws her arms in the air.

"A mulligan is a do-over," Hux says. "A mannigan is what every girl wants when a guy breaks up with her."

The girls punch and shove him. I don't scold. When they grow tired of battling, they resume their reading.

"And what's up with your hair?" Gianna points to my picture. "It looks awful."

All three lean over the paper, nearly knocking heads.

They are so stinking cute.

Their closeness reminds me of their childhood days, sparking simple yet unforgettable memories of them crowding the bathroom sink to help each other brush their teeth, sitting on the family room floor attempting to tie each other's shoes, or huddling around their play table teaching themselves to cut with scissors—although Hux did lob one pigtail off each of the girls, once.

But they would gather here at the kitchen table often, knees bent on chairs, forearms resting on tabletop, and faces close enough to feel each other's breath. Around this stained, scratched, and marred old slab, they whispered their secrets to each other, played board games on snowy afternoons, traded Halloween candy, inspected wondrous rock finds from the creek.

I smile. Sniff sentimental tears. I love it when my kids get along—even if it is at my expense.

Delanie hears my sniffles. "Oh, my God, what are you crying about now?"

My emotions are like jumping beans. They zig and zag inside me, and no one understands what sets them off—including me.

"This will make her stop." Hux's gaze has remained fixed on the paper. "Is that bird shit on your arm?"

And it does.

"Wait, what? Where?" My gaze follows his finger. He's pointing to a picture of me in the magazine. "No, that's froth. From the ball washer."

"The broken one?" Gianna leans in. "Right there?"

"You can see it?" I glance at the upper left-hand corner of the picture.

"It's behind Blake." Hux sets the tip of his finger on it.

"The article mentions Blake had to pay for the ball washer." Delanie grumbles this information as if she had to pay for it herself.

"It does?"

Hux resumes reading out loud, and I have to cover my ears halfway through because I don't want to ruin my good mood. I haven't actually read the articles. The fact that I'm in the news is impressive enough for me.

I'm a television and internet sensation.

Hux's deep voice slithers through my fingers, so I traipse into the family room and click on the TV to block out his words, but the station is set to the sports channel. Two announcers debate Blake's chances of winning some national tournament while a snapshot of him on bended knee is displayed on a screen between them. One announcer leans toward the picture. "Is that bird—"

I click it off.

"ForePlay, I mean SandTrap, don't be a poor sport," Hux calls to me. "Come back."

The three of them laugh, uproariously.

"Everyone knows I didn't trap Blake," I holler. "He had that ring in his golf bag for two months."

"You've even garnered the attention of the fashion world," Hux says. "Some famous woman is insulting you."

While I don't care what the sports pundits say about me, fashion is another matter. I drop my hands from my ears.

"She calls you a blonde bimbo."

I trudge back. "Who called me a blonde bimbo?"

"Some supermodel, Catherine Winsley."

"Give me that." I rip the magazine from him.

"Who is it?" Gianna wants to know.

Hux points to the paragraph, and I speed read down to her name. I've never understood why women criticize each other. Aren't we on the same team? We should stick together.

"There's her picture. You golfed with her." Gianna points to the next page.

"She's a supermodel?" I huff. "It's Call-me-Cat. We played on a foursome together in Columbus."

Delanie opens my computer, we google her name, and find she is a model—and well-paid at that. Her long legs jut out of bikini after bikini across the internet. I practically have to wipe the drool off Hux's face.

I slam my laptop shut to break his stare. "Call-me-Cat is Agnese's niece's friend."

"Rutger Rosy?" Gianna asks.

I've got to stop calling her by that nickname. Karma's clenched her teeth in my back. "Rosy's friend, yes."

"Cat doesn't like you." Hux returns to the article. "She doesn't like you a lot."

"Well, it's not like I'm hankering for a friend with half the brains of a Barbie doll, so I'm good."

"Ready to ride?" Blake's blaring voice startles us. He's leaning against the wall near the kitchen door, looking as if he's been listening for a while. A smile spans his face. "What are you looking at?"

"Oh, nothing." I step toward him. "I'm ready."

He rocks his chin from side to side and clicks his tongue against the side of his mouth, amusement combined with a reprimand. "I told you not to read the tabloids."

"But her picture's in an article. She's knocked her ball in the sand," Hux quips. The girls turn their backs, laughing.

"In a SandTrap?" Blake's eyes twinkle.

"Very funny." I grab my purse and shepherd him out of the room.

"If you haven't read this article yet, you need to, Blake," Hux hollers. "The pictures alone are hysterical. Mom has bird shit on her."

"That is not bird doo-doo." I keep pushing Blake toward the front door. I yell over one shoulder, "Rip that up."

We step outside, and I slam the door behind us so I can't hear Hux laugh. Blake and I have a date for a bike ride on the Erie peninsula today because of the doctor's instructions that I must cut back my running. Blake's worried I won't. He believes a long, leisurely bike ride will help curb my running appetite.

A warm breeze hits me as I step off my front porch. The flowers in my front yard bend in all four directions as the wind finds them, and the brightness of the blue sky and puffy white clouds soothes me. I erase the bad press from my thoughts. My conviction to enjoy a little cardio therapy escalates.

Then I hear a high-pitched crow.

"Hello." It's Kathy Gorney, who lives across the street. "Hi, Nikki, do you know you're in People magazine?"

"Good morning, Mrs. Gorney." I raise a hand, wiggle my fingers, and whisper to Blake without moving my lips. "We're in People, too?"

"Welcome to the wonderful world of golf." He plants a quick, soft kiss on my lips.

"Gee, thanks. I had no idea it was customary to stab the lousy players in the back after they finish playing."

"Only the ones who don't count their mannigans."

"How long were you listening?"

"Long enough to know I'm crazy about you." If it's possible to see love on someone's face, I see it now, dancing across Blake's.

"Yeah, well, the other players' wives don't like me."

"Who? Call-me-Cat? Ignore her. Her husband is the same way." He picks up my bag with my helmet, bike shoes, and gloves. "Is this the bag of the beautiful new bombshell wreaking havoc on the internet? I hear she's breaking hearts across the country because she's engaged to some undeserving third-class pro."

"Yep, that's me. I'm on the Science channel, too. A new show. *Forty-seven and Pregnant.*"

He laughs, slips his fingers into mine with his free hand, and we head toward the driveway. He's already mounted my bike on the top of his car, so he tosses my bag in the back, and I open my door. Out of the corner of my eye, I see Mrs. Gorney. She's shuffling down her driveway, slippers scuffing cement, waving her magazine in the air.

"Nikki," she crosses the street and presents the picture of Blake down on one knee. The photo is enlarged across two pages. She glances over both shoulders then whispers. "Is that bird poop on your arm?"

Blake tries to hide his laugh.

I sigh. Wasn't it just yesterday I complained about being ignored?

Careful what you wish for.

Chapter Twenty - The ride

Today we cruise toward Presque Isle State Park, Erie's greatest tourist-attraction. The peninsula stretches along Lake Erie's shore for six miles, carrying with it fresh-water beaches, a thirteen-mile loop road, a winding bike path, and a forest of green in between. The beauty of Presque Isle alone will make you forget your worries, which might be what Blake has in mind.

With our bikes perched on top of Blake's car, the windows cracked, and a tepid wind caressing our faces, my life seems near perfect. I haven't been this happy since—since never.

That the publicity surrounding me holds a negative overtone is the only imperfect feature in my world right now, but that will change. Blake's been in a public fishbowl for over a decade and insists the media goes up and down like a yo-yo.

"Before too much time passes, that pretty little pout of yours will bounce you to the top, compliments flowing," he promises as we speed along.

Yesterday, he dragged my old bike out of the garage attic and ferried it to a local bike shop along with his for a tune-up, so we could ride together.

He's hoping cycling will curtail my crazy running habit. He's promised to ride with me when he's able, and I've agreed to be obedient, divvy my limited running mileage up over three days and bike in between. How I deserve such a great guy, I'll never know.

My hormones must be dancing because tears fill my eyes.

"Are you okay?" He reaches across the front seat and grabs my hand.

"I'm more than okay," I say, squeezing his fingers.

A minute later, Blake pulls into a parking lot and readies our bikes. We slip on gloves and helmets and take off for some exercise.

Today, clouds billow over blue skies and sun, and we welcome the overcast when it comes because it eases the heat. We complete a mighty workout, riding around the entire peninsula at a good clip then decide to cycle the loop a second time. A quarter of the way around, Bennett calls Blake, and we pull over to find out what the emergency is.

"You're where? At the club?" I hear him say. He motions for me to edge farther off the road. I do, then I stand straddling my bike, listening. I gather from half of the conversation that Bennett and Evy are golfing at Blake's club today.

"Did they call Williams in?" he hollers into the phone, competing with the engines of passing cars.

After several moments of discussion in which I have no interest—I amuse myself by watching three baby geese float along the water behind their mother—Blake clicks the phone off and announces we have to head back.

"One of the pros who has lessons this afternoon came down with the flu. I'm going to cover for him. Think you can take me? Bennett said he can drop me at home when I'm done."

"You're not going home to change?'

"Not enough time. I'll shower at the club. I have plenty of clothes there."

"Okay," I agree.

"Just leave the bikes on the car, and I'll get them down when I get home."

"I can get—"

"Nikki." He inches his bike toward me, straddling the frame, then beckons for me with a finger. I lean toward him and he steals a kiss, smack on my lips. "There are lots of times in life I'll let you win, but this isn't one of them. You're not lifting anything, you hear me?"

"Okay, but you're overprotective. Lots of women have babies, Blake."

"You're not lots of women. You're my child's mother."

I like the sound of his concern. I smile as we mount our bikes and ride toward the car, my heart joyful that someone is pampering me for a change.

I'm in a good mood all the way to Blake's club. When Blake exits the car and I swing around to get into the driver's seat, he grasps my forearm. "Oh, wow, I forgot."

"Forgot what?"

"There are a ton of reporters hanging out in front of my house."

"Because of next week's tournament?"

"Yeah." He smiles. "That and this cute little blonde I've proposed to."

"Me? They're there because of me, too?"

He kisses me. "Don't worry. They won't bother you. They hang outside the driveway but won't trespass. Either give them a friendly wave or ignore them."

"I'll wave. I don't mind."

He shakes his head, laughing. "That's fine but don't answer any questions. No matter how badly that little mind of yours wants to."

He cups my chin in his hand, tilts my head, and kisses the tip of my nose.

"I won't," I promise.

I drive away, thrilled. Blake is used to reporters following him around, I'm not. The attention spices up my ordinary, boring life.

My mind wanders as I drive. This must be what movie stars deal with, paparazzi hounding them. People staking out their houses, jumping out of bushes, snapping pictures of you on beaches in skimpy bathing suits that make you look ten pounds heavier.

I square my shoulders and suck in my tummy, preparing. A chill claws its way from the pit of my stomach up to my hippocampus. I take a long, deep breath then have to pull to the side of the road and dig into my nausea satchel for a few crackers. I munch on them off and on for the remainder of the ride.

Rutger Rosy's words spring to mind. "You'll get used to it. Give them what they want, and they'll leave you alone."

If Rosy can do this, I can, too. I practice my smile in my rearview mirror at every stoplight. I wiggle my fingers out the driver's side window several times as I drive along. Once, a man waves back and I speed away. By the time I arrive in Blake's South Shore Drive neighborhood, I'm well-practiced and feeling swell about myself.

I turn onto Blake's street and there they are, the paparazzi. Four cars and a van line the curb in front of Blake's house. Inside my belly, the remains of my breakfast somersault, but I will myself not to throw up.

"I can do this," I promise, goosebumps running over my skin. An excitement I've never felt before climbs my spine.

As I approach, I notice one man in a shirt and tie, sporting a camera. He's chatting with another man dressed in a button-down shirt and khakis, who is leaning against the van, legs crossed at the ankles, arms tucked under armpits, and a camera dangling over one shoulder. He pushes off when he sees me coming, and both men lift their cameras to their faces. People exit the other cars. I take a deep breath and paste a fake, this-is-easy smile across my face.

I drive slowly, so I don't run over anyone's foot as they charge toward me. I wave and nod, remembering Rosy, acting thrilled to see them as if this is simply another normal day in Nikki Stone's spectacular life. I hit the garage door opener right before I turn into the driveway. I'm forced to slow almost to a stop because the van is parked so close to the entrance of Blake's driveway, making the turn tight. Cameras flash. A few photographers shout questions. Two cameramen walk alongside my moving vehicle, filming me through the driver's side window until I round the corner, and they halt in the street.

As soon as I'm safely riding over driveway pavers, my smile widens, and I speed toward the garage in Blake's fancy car. I'm pleased with myself, proud, and thanking fate that my mini media-blitz moment went so well. I clench the steering wheel, hands shaking, heart pounding with delight, and as I drive into the garage, there is an obscene crash and powerful jolt.

What was that?

I press on the gas pedal with my foot but something's restraining me. Some invisible force holds me captive. I glance in the rearview mirror wondering if a reporter has followed me in, but what could he be doing? Holding the bumper with the force of Superman? Behind me, they've gathered at the driveway's threshold, snapping pictures, filming, and—are they laughing?

I open the car door, shoving it hard because it, too, seems jammed. Right away I notice a looming shadow hovering above and behind me, to the rear of the car. I step out and glance upward. There, on the roof, Blake's and my bikes are mangled together in a heaping mass of metal, half inside, half outside the garage. The garage door is bent and off one side of its track.

Dazed by my stardom and absorbed by my imitation of Rutger Rosy, I'd forgotten the bikes were mounted on top.

I stand, remembering Mark, of all people. His words. "You're always getting yourself in these fixes," he said once after a golf lesson when he was forced to pick me up from the hospital. It was one of the first times I'd met Blake. He drove me there after I was knocked out by a golf ball.

Well, he knew up front of my bad luck.

But how many more ridiculous incidents can occur in one person's life?

Right then, fate answers. One side of a shelf on a side wall busts loose. Its board swings away from me and jugs of—of what? —some car lubricant slide toward me. I duck too late. The first bottle clips me in the shoulder, breaks open, and douses me with a black goop that smells gassy, thick, and putrid.

I squeeze my lips together but my mouth bulges despite my effort, and I projectile vomit onto Blake's lawn mower and workbench.

Perfect.

Chapter Twenty-one - The internet

By the weekend, I have a Twitter hashtag: #duckndriveNik.
"She's an internet sensation," Hux wails.

Why am I not jumping up and down? Isn't this what I wanted? To be noticed?

Hux and Evy stand in front of my big-screen TV in my family room. I sit at the kitchen table, trying not to watch. Hux has played the YouTube version of me driving the bikes into the garage door seven thousand times.

"Your dream, manifested." Evy cups an elbow with one hand and sips coffee as he watches. "In living, breathing, disconcerting color."

"Not exactly what I'd hoped."

"Careful what you wish for." Evy is a wonderful friend. Except when he isn't.

"I wish you'd stop saying that."

"Evy's right, Mom. You were always crying about being ignored. Now everyone knows your name. DuckndriveNik."

"I wasn't crying about it."

I'm trying to decide whether I'm mildly tickled or elaborately traumatized by my newborn popularity. People left twenty-nine messages on my home phone last night, filling its memory, an additional twenty-one in voice mails on my cell, and another two hundred and fifty-three texts. Of course, one-fourth of the texts were scathing messages from my children, the girls chastising and Hux reminding me what a complete idiot I am.

Apparently, I should have made another one of my prayers, "I want to be noticed," more specific.

Lesson learned.

"I bet she hits a million by next week."

"What does she have now?" Evy leans over Hux's shoulder, glimpsing his phone.

"Over four hundred thousand." I'm beginning to hate that high-pitched whine of Hux's. "And five hundred and fifty-nine comments."

"Five, five, nine." Evy leans away, turns back to the TV. "You should play that number, Naggy. Are those your new cycling shorts?"

He's referring to the shorts I'm wearing on the television.

"Yes." I pick up my toast and bite, attempting to quiet my stomach. I'm unsure why, if I'm past four months' gestation, the nausea hasn't slowed a smidge. "Ruined."

"The shirt, too?"

"Of course."

Hux rewinds the tape to the point where the oil drops from a ceiling shelf, breaks open, and douses me.

"Shame." Evy walks to the kitchen and takes a seat beside me, plopping his boney elbows on my table. He thumbs through Twitter with one hand and sips gas-station coffee with his other. I've been so nauseated lately, I set my Keurig on the back patio yesterday. Now everyone has to bring their own.

"You have a handful of new nicknames. Care to hear them?"

"No, thanks. And can you move back? Your coffee's making me sick."

"When do you go to the doctor again?"

"Next week."

"Why'd she put a kibosh on your California trip with Blake? Because of the nausea?"

Blake contacted Doctor Yank the minute he was invited to a California tournament. Of course, she insisted my traveling was out of the question.

"No, because of my age. She said I have to be cautious."

"Maybe she'll release your chains when you're a little further along."

"That's another thing. She doesn't think I'm as far along as originally believed. Because I'm still sick."

"You've lost weight."

"Yeah."

"Again, careful what you—"

"Stop."

"All right. All right. Calm down. Don't ballyhoo yourself into giving birth. What should you chant? Huff, huff, exhale, or something? Speaking of. Are you and Blake taking birthing classes?"

This statement sends Hux screeching. "Oh, my God, birthing classes. You and Blake and a bunch of twenty-year-old couples sitting cross-legged."

An image of Blake and me huffing on the floor alongside a boy whose underwear peeks over his jeans and a girl chewing gum hits me. I'm big as a water buffalo. Class ends. Everyone skips away except me. I can't get off the mat.

"Good morning, Gianna." Evy's salutation rescues me from my visualization.

Gianna walks stiffly by me, lifting a piece of toast off my plate as she passes. She shoves it in her mouth then scurries to the refrigerator, reaches in, shuffles food, and grabs a Coke. Right before she leaves the kitchen, she tosses the toast in the garbage. "Who eats toast without butter?"

"That better not be the last Coke," I warn.

She ignores me, tramps out the door, and I wave a hand after her. "See?" I say to Evy. "Still invisible."

To prove my point, Delanie prances into the room, says, "Hi Evy," and stuffs her purse with bottled water and yogurt.

"C'mere. Watch the guy on the left." Hux waves her over, and suddenly her deafness is cured. She meanders toward him, and he replays the video, stopping at the point where I drive smack into the garage. "The one snapping pictures. He nearly drops his camera."

Hux restarts the video in slow motion, points, and the two of them laugh at the guy bungling his camera in the background. With a few taps, the man gets hold of it before it hits the ground.

"Nice save," Delanie chuckles. They've watched this clip a hundred times, searching for new antics.

"Wait. Here it comes. Read the guy's lips right after Mom pukes." Hux sets a hand on her arm to keep her from leaving. The two of them laugh until they cry.

"What did he say?" I holler.

"He's saying, 'What an f'ing disaster.'"

Ugh.

"Are you happy now? No more wallflower. Everyone knows your name." Evy straightens in his seat. "Wasn't there a tavern like that? Where everyone knew everyone's name?"

"Yeah. A bar. I wish I was there, so I could have a drink." I sip Coke. "Hopefully, this fades before the entire world sees it."

"A major chunk of the American population already has." He sets his coffee cup down, still thumbing through Twitter. "The comments are getting nasty."

"Will you put that down, please?"

He continues thumbing, ignoring me. "So Doctor Yank hasn't established a due date?"

"Not yet. She will after the sonogram."

In the background, Hux clicks off YouTube and turns on the TV. Deep voices of announcers reverberate through my house. I ignore them even when Delanie and Hux both let out gasps. Evy jumps up to see what's going on, and I collect the dirty dishes the kids left on the table at midnight last night, rinse them in the sink, and load them into the dishwasher, wondering how I've grown into my mother's role, constantly cleaning up after kids. Mom never divvied out chores to Barb and me. Unlike me, she was content to do them on her own.

"Why don't you give your girls chores?" her friend Beverly asked once.

I remember the soft lines of Mom's face shifting upward. "Because they'll have the rest of their lives to clean up after others."

At the time I thought, "Phew. Way to go, Mom." Now I understand the magnitude of her statement, figuratively and literally—the blood, sweat, and tears of child-rearing.

I set a hand on my belly and hope this baby will remember me as fondly as I remember her, appreciate my maternal sacrifices more than his or her older siblings.

I drop soap in the dishwasher, start it up, and glance toward the family room. Everyone has stopped laughing.

"Mom?" Hux turns. His expression reveals something's wrong. He has that surprised look someone has after they've been slapped. "Who's Larry?"

Chapter Twenty-two - The rumor

I hate roller coasters. Riding up and down, twirling around, the anticipation of the upcoming fall stifling you on your way up, fear rushing through you on your way down, the sheer terror your seat belt will unbuckle paralyzing you throughout.

I'm no fonder of life's undulating ride. Twenty-four hours ago, I wallowed in happiness; now I stand stunned in front of the TV alongside Evy, Hux, and Delanie, watching a whirlpool of deceit unfold.

My own.

I wanted to be noticed. Prayed for someone, anyone, to see me as more than a simple, mundane mom. Ultimately, now they do but for the wrong reason. My lie has come back to haunt me.

A local newscaster, Paul Eckendorf, either mistakenly or deviously revealed Lawrence's name, suggesting a love triangle exists between Larry, Blake, and me. He's on our local news relaying faulty proof of a sordid love affair and looking way too happy about it. He's referring to me as a Fairview divorcee on the prowl.

"When I told you God said to love one another, I didn't mean in the bedroom," Evy scolds.

"You know I would never sleep with Lawrence," I contest. *This is the worst thing in the world.*

In his newscast, Eckendorf insinuates a paternity test is needed.

"What will people think of me?"

What will Jack Bruno think? Mark? My neighbors? My ninety-year-old nana? Eckendorf dumps his tasteless "food for thought" editorial into a great big bowl of local shaming. He suggests my baby is Lawrence's and I'm blackmailing Blake.

My cell rings and I answer it only because it's Sherry. She's seen the lascivious report, too. We concur: This has Agnese written all over it.

Whether Agnese or her heinous niece suggested Lawrence as the possible father of my baby is immaterial. Clearly, Agnese overheard the conversation between Sherry and me, misconstrued or flat out lied about the situation, and either she told Paul or she told Rutger, who told Paul, and he unprofessionally blabbed it on his local editorial newscast.

Hux clicks through the sports channels. Thankfully, this hasn't leaked to the national broadcasts. Yet.

After my initial shock, my reaction shifts sympathetically toward Lena. If this mortifies me, how does she feel? Would she believe Lawrence and I slept together? Having been the laughingstock of the Fairview community when my husband fathered a child by another woman, I can guess how she must feel. I pray the stab of gossip for her versus the bludgeoning truth I experienced penetrates less deeply.

Why do these things keep happening to me?

My mind sifts through a myriad of reasons, but I cannot understand what I do to attract this chaos. Normally, I leave existentialism to Evy. He insists like attracts like, and after the kids leave, he follows me around, reminding me of this while I prepare to drive to Lena's. I can't call her. I have to talk to her in person.

I grab a red sweater from the front closet and catch a glimpse of myself in the mirror by the front door. I remind myself of Scarlett O'Hara. I shiver.

Where am I going? To Ashley's birthday party?

I rip it off and grab a thin cream-colored jacket.

"You subliminally manifest calamity," Evy says over my shoulder. "And I like the red sweater better."

"This isn't my fault," I retort, though it might be. I initiated the stud-daddy Larry rumor. "And I'm not wearing red."

"Why not concentrate on what's important in life instead of wallowing in sorrow for yourself because you are an unappreciated mother. That's how this all began. You'd lure less trial and tribulation if you stop the self-pity."

"Evy, I'm a working mom who's neglected like millions of other moms out there. Don't slough this off as if it's a menial moral mistake."

"Here's an idea: Treat yourself to a pedicure next time you feel ignored, not a woe-is-me revelry that attracts ruin. You could have gotten that pretty coral color you love and felt better about yourself."

"This isn't as simple for women as it is for men."

"That's discriminatory."

He follows me upstairs where I change my clothes into simple jeans and a white shirt. I want to look as bland and innocent as possible.

"When women stay at home, people treat them like second-class citizens, and when they work, people say we shirk our motherhood duties. There's no winning. No matter what we do, we are unappreciated. Now people will say I'm a loose woman."

"Change underneath."

"What? It's not that simple."

He shakes his head. "Your pink bra. If you don't want to look like a hussy, lose the pink bra."

I grab a neutral bra, run into the bathroom, and change. I come out fighting. "No one considers my wants and needs. I'm surrounded by a golf pro, his kids, my kids, friends, and a wide assortment of coworkers, all of whom have their own set of—what did you call their troubles?"

"Trials and tribulations?"

"With their own trials and tribulations. I'm trying to sort it out, but catastrophes follow me around all day."

"You got one thing right. Nothing is simple about you. You're in a class by yourself."

"My struggles don't differ from other mothers'." I compare myself to them quickly in my head then add, "I'm just a scant clumsier."

"You could give Lucille Ball a run for her money in the clumsy department."

I ignore this.

"Correct me if I'm wrong," I contend. "Our grandmothers took medication to survive their housewife status. That's why our generation works."

"Valium."

"What?"

"They took Valium."

"Whatever."

"And only because it was cheaper than fine wine."

"What I'm saying, Evy, is women are beastly, back then and now, but occasionally we need something to boost us through those—what's that again?

"Trials and tribulations."

"Right."

"Men need as much support as women," he argues.

"Let me remind you, a man broadcasted this rumor."

While I tidy up my house, Evy and I skip into a debate on which sex is better, male or female. He follows me around with a white glove, judging both my poor housekeeping and opinions on gender. I contend women are harder working than men and squabble that Evy doesn't understand us. Women are the compassionate gender. (Okay, that sounds discriminatory.) We pour our heart and soul into our relationships, so sometimes, inadvertently, we allow friends, family, coworkers, or mere acquaintances to take advantage of us.

"We are recklessly loyal."

I embark on a lecture about the loyalty of sisterhood, hurrying because I have to get to Lena's house fast. Evy reminds me that one of my working "sisters" lied to scumbag Paul about me and Lawrence. I shoo him out the door without replying, and he leaves my house with a sense of triumph. I allow his victory only because I'm rushed. I clean myself up and head toward Lena's and Lawrence's before they hear the news.

I may not know Lena well, but I like her. She's humble and kindhearted. She will live out her life hurting few people, and I don't want her to hurt, either. In one afternoon of shopping and a few follow-up phone calls, a budding sisterhood has blossomed between us.

Last week, she called, thanking me for helping her pick out new clothes and giggling that Larry loved them. She disclosed they've been getting along fabulously, better than in years, and she has me to thank for it.

I pray she doesn't believe the rumors.

On the way to her house, Blake calls and I pull to the side of the road and explain what was on the local news. He insists the rumor will hit major networks within hours.

"You should tell her in person," he advises.

"I'm on my way there now."

"Good."

We share silence for a moment. Then he asks apprehensively, "Can you fend for yourself for another few days?"

"Did you get into that Canadian tournament?"

He's spending today, Saturday, through Wednesday in Milwaukee on an eleventh-hour tourney. His last win escalated his rank. A revolving door of tournament directors contacts him daily, inviting him to play at their matches.

"I did. I can come home on Thursday if you need me," he replies. "But if you can handle the media on your own, my PR guy would like to update some of my professional photos and have me do a few interviews in Canada."

"No, no, no. I can handle them." I'm not sure of this, but I'm still hung up on being the perfect girlfriend/fiancée. "You go ahead."

"Are you sure?"

"I'm positive."

"Okay, but don't tune in to newscasts. And don't read the tabloids. These things blow up and fizzle out. Ignore them."

Blake doesn't listen to opinion polls or sportscasts. He hardly sweats the small stuff. He's been a star for years, and now his twinkle has magnified. Every game he plays and stroke he takes is examined, analyzed, and either praised or criticized. Yet he takes this in stride with the temperament of the Dalai Lama.

I, on the other hand, have broken into successive clothes-ruining perspiration bouts in the past few weeks. My itty-bitty budding existence of forty-seven years has been lost in a colorful bouquet of successful women. I was a dandelion amidst sunflowers, hidden in the shadows of dazzling, long-stemmed, golden-rayed beauties like Rutger Rosy and Call-me-Cat. I had to claw my way up the stems around me with a vengeance, and as soon as my peewee petals opened up, finally blooming, people noticing, the grim reaper strikes. Plows down my yellow bracts. Thrusts me into the dirt.

"Don't do any interviews," Blake adds, then after a long silence, he brings my dance with insecurity to an abrupt end. "Nikki, tell me again. For peace of mind."

"Tell you what?"

"That I don't need to worry about this Larry guy."

I can't help myself. I snort a laugh. "Blake, first of all, I am so ridiculously in love with you that you never have to worry about another man ever again as long as you live, and, secondly, Lawrence is a great guy but he is not for me. As soon as you come home, we are going over to his house, and you'll see for yourself. I promise."

I can't believe I have to reassure him, the handsome, adored golf pro. Then I remember. The last woman he loved cheated on him.

"I'm running late," he says. "I have to go. I love you. Good luck with Lena."

The conversation ends, and I shove the shift into drive, head with my bucket of water toward the next fire, wishing Evy were there so I could say, "See the flames raging around me? We women battle blazes all day long."

I bite my lip, fret, worry, and hyperventilate as I drive tortoise-like toward Lena's house. My legs are shaking when I walk up the path to her front porch. Before I ring the bell, the door swings open and I come face to face with her.

"I saw the news," she says, her expression sober, angry.

I hold my breath. I can't speak.

"Those lousy, lying scoundrels. How can I help, Nikki?"

I release the chilly wind in my lungs, burst into tears, and throw my arms around her. "You just did."

I stand crying in her arms on the porch.

Chapter Twenty-three - The sonogram

Doctor Yank taps away on her iPad, her expression stern. "I'll schedule a sonogram for Friday."

Despite being fully dressed, the exam table's stiff cushion beneath me is no more comfortable today than any other day. Around me the room's pale-yellow color glares at me, reflecting off two fluorescent ceiling lights that are too long for the room. The ambience of her entire office is as unwelcoming as Doctor Yank's surly face.

You'd think they'd at least pretty up these torture chambers.

Earlier in the week, I called to ask if there was a safe medication I could take for nausea because it seems so much worse lately, and the nurse insisted on scheduling an emergency appointment.

"Could we do the sonogram on Thursday?" I request. I'm not sure Blake will travel home for the sonogram, but I want to make it an option.

Dr. Yank scowls as if I'm a kid asking for my succor too soon. I rush to say, "Blake is out of town but there is a chance he may be home on Thursday."

Her face brightens.

"Oh. Yes. That's doable." She hesitates, eyes to the ceiling, as if I've asked when it's convenient for her to meet with him. I'm learning to drop his name when needed. "I'll sneak you in. Would he be available, say, three fifteen?"

Who am I? Heidi Fleiss?

"Sure."

"Great. Wonderful," she replies, then her face hardens. "In the meantime, rest. You've been through a lot in the past few days with the media. Your stomach issues could be the result of recent—inconveniences."

For a second, I thought she was about to say infidelity. I'm surprised she hasn't offered a free paternity test.

"Ms. Stone—"

Oh no, please don't.

"By testing your blood and swabbing Blake's mouth, you can halt the scandalous chatter."

Bingo.

"You're suggesting a paternity test?" I think I'm psychic.

Her face reddens. "DNA test. Yes. If the rumors are upsetting. You must concentrate on your well-being and the health of the baby."

And Blake. Don't forget Blake.

"And I'm sure this isn't good for a professional golf player's state of mind, either." She smiles.

I am psychic.

"Blake knows he's the father." I return a quick, curt smile.

"Of course, of course." She backpedals, attempts to recoil her unprofessionalism. "I suggested this purely to calm media attention."

Give me a break.

I cannot believe this woman is going to deliver my baby. She'll be swooning over Blake while my kid slips through her fingers and onto the floor.

"I'm simply saying," she adds when I don't respond. Before she continues, she stops, her shoulders relax, and she sets her iPad down. "Look, you can't lose any more weight. Not an ounce. You've lost more than five percent of your body weight. We've got to get you to hold your food down."

This is the first time she's let her professional guard down and talked with me frankly, and while that should elate me, it scares me. This weight loss problem must be serious. Despite my protruding belly, I've lost another two pounds this week. I'm not sure if I'm peeing or throwing up more these days.

"You don't think—" I swallow deeply, force the toast and crackers halfway up my throat back down into my belly. "I'm not miscarrying, am I?"

"Let's not worry about a miscarriage. Every pregnancy is different. Some women are sick for nine months. At your age, however, we should be cautious. I don't want you losing any more weight."

I've been so consumed with my sudden stardom and dousing the fires of rumor, I haven't considered the importance of this life inside me. I haven't worried I might lose this child.

How could I be so selfish?

Doctor Yank must see the remorse in my face. Her voice softens. "Try eating smaller meals several times a day. I know it can be difficult when you're nauseated. I want you to stop and see Emily, our dietician, before you leave today. Then we'll see you back here on Thursday." She finishes tapping and wraps up my appointment with a sympathetic stroke of my arm and smile. Then just like that, her spark of compassion and female comradery combusts. "With Blake."

Of course.

Ten minutes later, the dietician hands me a packet of information, pages through it with me, and sends me on my way. By the time I'm in the car, I realize I haven't listened to a word the dietician uttered. Once I'm home, I read my instructions: intersperse snacks of toast, crackers, plain nuts, and yogurt, which makes me sick when I'm pregnant. Just reading "yogurt" sends me running to the bathroom.

I take the remainder of the day off and indulge in an afternoon nap. Before and after my snooze, I eat as many bland cookies and muffins as I can hold down.

Blake calls and ecstatically agrees to travel home for the sonogram. He can't hide his excitement. With so many girls in both our families, I'm sure he's secretly betting on the odds that we have a boy. I let him know they may not be able to tell the sex of the baby yet—we already discussed it and decided we do want to know—but he said he wouldn't miss this regardless.

He has limited time but has no problem connecting flights. Even airlines dote over him. He mentioned he was going home for a sonogram to the woman checking him in, and she upgraded him to first class for free.

What's that old Brad Paisley song say? "The more they run my name down, the more my price goes up." Something like that. "No matter what you do," blah, blah, blah, "people think you're cool." Blake's Twitter followers rose from 45,000 to 162,000 over the weekend.

I click on my phone and check. Today his count has soared past 200,000. Yesterday's hot trend was #IsBlaketheDaddy and #whoisLarry.

Lawrence-not-Larry is loving the secretive, spicy fame. Lena, too. They've promised to keep out of everything until the time is right. Blake can't meet them this trip because he will only be here hours, but we have a dinner scheduled for the end of next week—provided no other tournament directors call begging and provided I'm feeling up to it.

Instead of gaining strength, I've become sicker by the day. I pray this is due to my nerves.

On Monday morning, the Larry rumor hits ESPN. Even Savannah Guthrie mentions my name on the Tuesday Today Show.

I do have to admit that gave me a thrill. Savannah's my idol. She's brutally smart with beastly interviewing skills, yet she's clumsy, although Carson Daly told Blake she's massively competitive. I've held an adoring comradery with her—a klutzy-sisterhood connection—from afar. That she referred to me as the sainted Blake Anderson's little wedge in the sand does not break the chains of female infatuation. Carson Daly got out of sorts over her remark. Carson loves Blake. They've golfed together many times.

Despite everyone wanting to know who Larry is, so far no pictures have materialized. They've flashed lots of Blake and me. Blake looking fine. Me, frazzled. Once I had vomit on my shirt, and, of course, the bird doo-doo pic made it to last night's ESPN

Sports Tip of the Day. The announcer quipped, "Blake, old boy, get off that knee and head down to Walgreens. Paternity tests are on sale. Ninety-nine bucks. That's all for tonight…"

Blake doesn't mention a single broadcast when he steps off the plane. He's so excited over the sonogram that he hurries me out of the terminal, we jump in the car, and I drink the test's required 32-ounces of water in the waiting room of the doctor's office. I'll have to drop him back at the airport in four hours, but luckily, Erie is small, so it's a mere fifteen-minute drive.

"I see you made it," Doctor Yank says when she bursts into the room.

Once again, I'm subjected to her infatuation with Blake. She asks if I've drunk the required water without looking at me.

"She has," Blake answers, smiling, and Doctor Yank skips into a lengthy documentary about what will take place. Blake confirms we want to know the baby's gender because, at this point, she's directing her instructions and questions toward him, not me.

With the shop talk complete, she washes her hands and pegs him with several golf questions. Meanwhile, I try not to pee my pants. I'm so waterlogged I feel like my back molars are about to float down my throat.

Blake must see the discomfort in my eyes because he politely mentions he's anxious to find out if the baby is a boy or a girl. He winks at me when Doctor Yank turns her back to retrieve her stool, probe, and gel. She giggles immaturely when she squeezes too much gel over my stomach and has to sop some of it up with paper towels.

She hits switches and the screen monitor lights up, a nurse enters, and Blake and I gaze at a garbled black and white picture that makes the baby look more monster than human. Doctor Yank moves the probe around my stomach, pushing and snapping pictures, pressing so hard I think I will pee.

The screen is tilted slightly away from us, so we can't see it well. The nurse steps in for a better view and in perfect sync, both of their happy faces slowly disintegrate, like ice cubes in coffee.

"Oh, my." Doctor Yank presses harder in several spots.

"What's wrong?" I snap. Blake squeezes my hand.

"Nothing. Nothing," she says, too quickly.

She turns to the nurse, mentions something about smelling salts, and blood barrels through every vein and capillary in my body.

I spent last evening sorting through old baby pictures of Delanie, Hux, and Gianna, recalling their first few twinges of life inside me. I stilled, waiting patiently, prayerfully, for movement. Could I feel her? Him?

Later, a tiny tingle vibrated in my tummy, answering my prayers, proving a distinct little personality formed inside me while I carried on, making my mark in the world. Elation swept through me. I pledged to remain calm from then on, realizing I was ecstatic to have another child—Blake's child. Knowing this itty-bitty person inside was the result of our love overwhelmed me, and I lay in my bed crying so hard that Furgy jumped up to see what was the matter.

Now, this can't be bad news. It just can't.

My epilepsy condition claws its way out of the back of my mind where I've buried it. The nurse rushes out the door, and my heart speeds up like the final fast ticks of a bomb about to blow.

"What's going on?" Blake's voice is shaking.

"Just procedural," the doctor replies, then the nurse returns with a second nurse, and again I think, this can't be happening. I begin praying.

Hail Mary, full of grace, please protect my baby.

Blake squeezes my hand so hard my fingers turn white.

"Nikki." Doctor Yank looks me straight in the eye. Both nurses stare at me. I know it is bad—so bad I've stolen the limelight from Blake.

"I think I'm going to pass out," I cry.

For the past month, I've made weekly stops at the doctor's office, so a nurse can check my blood levels. I'm on a low dose of medication for my epilepsy, and I've forced myself not to think about how it might affect my baby. Could something be wrong?

"You're fine," she replies, still pushing on my stomach. "Breathe. Steady. Don't let us lose you."

The nurse with the smelling salts plays with the packet.

"What's wrong with my baby?" I tremble.

"Calm down. You're fine. It's just—"

Unable to take her hesitation any longer, I scream, "What is it? Tell me."

"There's a second heartbeat."

My own heart skips a beat. Or two. Or three.

"Excuse me?"

"Breath in through the nose, out through the mouth," she says.

"Are you okay, Ms. Stone?" nurse number one asks. She whispers to the doctor that I'm losing my coloring.

"Twins?" Blake asks in a disturbingly monotone voice. "We're having twins?"

I glance at him. He's as white as I feel.

"No, no, no," I turn frantically back to Doctor Yank. "You're wrong."

"Ms. Stone—"

"I can't have twins. That's too many."

"In through the nose, out through the mouth," the second nurse moves forward and places a hand on my shoulder.

"I already have three," I say. "Blake has two. That would be—" I lean forward, trying to see the monitor better. "Look again. God wouldn't do that to me."

"Twins?" Blake repeats.

Doctor Yank holds her hand steady for a moment. "It can be shocking, I know."

"Oh, you know? Do you have twins? Are you forty-fricken-seven? Listen to me, Doctor Yank—"

"Who?" I vaguely hear one nurse ask the other.

I stab the air toward Doctor Yank with a pointed finger of my free hand. "I am not having twins."

She whispers to nurse number one, "Do you have the smelling salts ready?"

"I'm not fainting." I'm gritting my teeth so fiercely that I spit a little. "I'm—I'm objecting."

Blake has gone into shock. He keeps repeating the same four words to no one. "Did she say twins?"

"I want a second opinion." I'm losing control. "I'm too old to have twins."

"Did she say—?"

"Yes, Blake." I wiggle my hand free from his because it's gone numb.

"Twins?" He grabs my hand, harder. A kid afraid to leave his mother.

"Yes, Blake. I mean no."

I turn my anger to Doctor Yank. Blake keeps asking, squeezing. The doctor keeps nodding. The nurses keep leaning, waiting for me to faint. "Are you telling me?" I try to manage the volume of my voice while at the same time bring Dr. Yank to her senses. "Inside my forty-seven-year-old body, you see a second baby?"

"Yes, look here." She whirls the probe around on my stomach and faces the monitor toward me. I pee a little but don't care. "Here is one pulsing heart."

Her hand travels back and forth slowly and, oh, my God, I can see the second bleeping before she points it out…and…

This cannot be happening.

"Here is the second heartbeat."

Oh no, oh no, oh no. Don't say it. I can see it. The—

Both nurses step forward, closing in on me, the one ready to shove her little packet under my nose.

"And here is—" Doctor Yank looks like a ghost. "The third."

The room shuts down. Quiet.

Then:

"What?" Blake speaks first, snapped back to his senses.

"No, no, no, no, no." I lift my head off the pillow. "What did you say?"

There is a vague, third thumping on the screen. I can see it but can't believe it. My eyes skip from face to face to face to face, frantically searching for someone who will tell me I'm wrong. That there aren't three heartbeats.

I'm not sure what I look like, but it can't be worse than how Blake or the stymied nurses and doctor look.

Doctor Yank counts again, stupefied. One…two…three… She points. Her lips fall apart, and her face sags into a stare. Spittle forms on one corner of her mouth. She can't believe what she's seeing, either.

She's unfamiliar with my luck.

"You didn't," she utters from behind a forlorn face, "take fertility drugs, did you?"

"Are you crazy?"

I might be having an out-of-body experience. For a second, I'm floating. Up, up, up, away from this nightmare. My back brushes against the ceiling as some poor, horribly unlucky woman digests horrendous news on a table beneath my feet. Everyone in the room is astounded. A man slumps in a chair beside her. Two nurses cringe. The doctor keeps tapping the monitor's three pulsating specs like a confused mathematician.

I glimpse the face of the woman with the big belly, who is reclining on the ugly green table with the long white paper sheet and realize she's me. I swoosh back into my body and hear the sound of my voice bouncing off four walls. "I. Cannot. Be having— What? Are you? Saying? Am I having—?"

"Triplets." She says the word I can't bring myself to utter.

Blake's fingers slip away from mine. I lean to the side of the bed and throw up on the sonogram machine, then as I fall back onto the examining table, I hear a loud thud, glance to the other side of the bed, and see Blake on the floor—out cold.

Chapter Twenty-four - The acceptance

We have no time to grasp the magnitude of our situation. I rush Blake to the emergency room, and they stitch the v-shaped gash on the corner of his forehead where he hit the edge of the examining table as he fell. During the course of both the trip to the hospital and the drive to the airport, neither of us speak. We're in shock. We had been preparing to become a family of seven. Ten sounds so much more frightening.

We'll be sixty when these…kids—I can't utter the T-word—are teenagers.

Once we arrive at the airport, Blake asks six times if I'm sure I'm all right if he leaves. He punctuates his fifth and sixth inquisitions with an "I can opt out of this tournament." Where usually, I'm a blubbering crybaby grabbing at any sleeve within reach for sympathy, right now I want to be alone.

For the first time in my lonely life, I'm crowded.

In a zombie-like daze, much like his, I reassure Blake six times I'm fine and he kisses me goodbye, holding me without speaking for an excruciatingly long minute. I don't watch him walk inside. Instead, I speed away as if he's the one pregnant, and I'm making a getaway.

Is that how he feels?

I drive for a while, turn down an unfamiliar street, heading toward Lake Erie, and pull into a parking space where I can see the waves sweeping against the shoreline. Unlike me, the lake is calm today, and I long to drink in its tranquility, lap up its simple, unfailing existence. I crack the window, set my head back, close my eyes, and listen to soft water caressing sand.

I tap my fingers together just to feel something physical. I evaluate myself. My heart has slowed to a normal pace. My legs feel taut and strong, not achy as usual because I've cut out my long runs. I have a mild headache, but it's manageable. My hands and feet have lost their tingling of an hour ago. My stomach mimics the lake—calm, not a drop of nausea.

I don't know how this calmness has come over me. Survival? Or surrender?

When I was young, before Mark, before the kids, before days began zipping by at a blazing pace, I looked at life as a puzzle with intricate pieces that snapped perfectly together, but motherhood, love, friendship, and work dimmed that big picture.

Before Delanie and Hux and Gianna, I had dreams. So many dreams. I imagined my puzzle with brilliant, dazzling pieces of pink, yellow, orange, opaque white, and Caribbean blue. What exciting opportunities lay before me? What path would materialize by snapping the pieces together? Law school dangled as an idea at one corner. A high-profile business CFO at another. A physician? An engineer? I wanted to have a presence. Make a name for myself in the world while being this magnificent mother who would raise caring, compassionate kids. I'd volunteer at soup kitchens, donate to women's rights causes. I'd be a person people noticed when I walked by. They'd say, "There goes Nikki Stone. She's wildly successful."

But time slipped past me. I became this lost person in a sea of lost people. One in a million mothers and an accountant, of all things. There was no one more boring than me. Then along came Blake.

I had to fall in love with a superstar to remind myself of my paltry existence. People knock me over to get to him, barely acknowledging my presence, and if I'm not lost in Blake's stardom then I'm hovering in my kids' shadows.

Is there enough love inside me? To step aside and care for three more people?

Right now, I'm a social media joke, and it's sure to get worse. When news hits the stand that I'm carrying triplets, I'll be the butt of everyone's jokes.

I wish I had the faith of my mother. Believed that "this too shall pass." That the press will realize Blake is truly the father, and the forty-something, carrying-triplets, sure-to-storm-the-airwaves story will die down. Unfortunately, it will take some poor soul falling flat on his or her face to send the newscasters scurrying away from my door.

When the glare does dim, Blake will leave for his tournaments; Delanie, Hux, and Gianna will be gone, snapping their puzzle pieces into place; and I'll remain at home, alone, with three itsy-bitsy people, whom I know nothing about.

Is it possible to rejoice and mourn at the same time?

By forty-seven, I had clawed my way up the shadowy side of the motherhood mountain, stood victoriously at the top, the wind at my back, and had begun my descent, skipping down a clear path, basking in the sunshine, financial security, a great new job, and the freedom to come and go as I pleased.

Now a squall has scooped me up, whirled me around, and plummeted me back where I began. Only this time as I labor up the hill, my legs aren't as strong, my mind not as sharp, and my determination is worn. I've snapped more than half of life's pieces into my puzzle, some with bright hues. What remains are bland, boring, and blanched—dreams dashed.

I'll be Blake's wife. Delanie's, Hux's, Gianna's, triplet one's, triplet two's (*Oh, my God!*), and triplet number three's mother.

I don't have enough love to go around.

The frightening truth that dawns on me is that I'm an extraordinarily ordinary mother. I'll never stand out in life, never accomplish anything exceptional. I'm a nameless face in a big corral of underappreciated, undervalued, overworked moms. Kids will continue to rush by me, grabbing food from my plate, ignoring my rules, poking fun at me, and texting secret names for me to their friends. On the golf course, I'll be a person applauding in a crowd, a pro's wife, what's-her-name, the mother of Blake Anderson's children, stepmother of his girls, always someone else's something.

I close my eyes and remember my dreams. They disappear one by one. Traveling, empty nesting with the complete freedom to come and go as I please, purchasing a cute little convertible (okay, that's a dumb one), moving into the CFO's office—

I gasp.

My job. I realize how ecstatic and excited I was about becoming Bruno's CFO. I can't accept the position now. I'm not sure I'll be able to work at all for the next year or two or fifteen.

Panic rises in my soul, and just as quickly, a soothing voice from the past, my mother's, slithers inside my head, ferrying wisdom. "*God never gives you more than you can bear. Accept what he hands you and do your best.*"

What if my best isn't good enough? What if I can't care for three more human beings? What if there isn't enough love left inside of me to divide up and still be a good mom? How much love is an individual expected to give? How much self-denial? I worry bitterness may overtake me. Mattering is human nature. I want to matter.

But you do, Nikki, you truly do. In so many ways. Can't you see the pieces of your life fitting together?

I recline my seat so that the rays of the setting sun filter through my window and touch my tired mind. I close my eyes, allow the rhythm of the waves to soothe me.

I have to change. It isn't the kids or Blake or Mark or anyone else who can make me feel better about my life—it's me. It's not them who see me as worthless. It's me.

The images of the people I love form in my head. Blake's dimple surfacing during the first private lesson I took with him. The twinkle in Hux's eye in that snapshot of him golfing off the rooftop of our house. (Yes, he did, and he convinced me to golf off the roof, too.) I remember the fierce warmth of Delanie's arms around me when she first heard Mark had fathered a child by another woman. And I recall the long talk with Gianna during the divorce. When kids at school teased her about her illegitimate sister, she rallied and created a no-bullying campaign, which still exists today.

These three babies will bring with them a myriad of beautiful images, too, but how hard will the crosses be in their lives? How much will I have to endure—for them?

Devastation isn't half as hard to bear when it happens to you compared to when something or someone hurts your child.

I open my eyes. One of my greatest traits is my ability to protect my children, to place them before myself, but I must be honest. I can't raise three more kids alone. Blake will help, but the bulk of the work—and I can't fathom how labor-intensive triplets will be—is going to fall to me.

Daylight slips from the sky, but instead of dimming, my vision clears.

The sun sets and the waves lap and the evening's shadows rise around me, magnifying dusk's colors. A rainbow of vivid hues spread across the horizon like sweet, stretched taffy, and my soul tastes and sips the nectarous calmness of the hour.

A golden ray slips through my windshield and falls across my face, warming me. I know what I must do.

I don't have to be spectacular. I just have to be—enough.

I can't be more than I am. Like most mothers, I make demands of myself that I would never place on anyone else. But now it's time to ask for help.

I lift my cell off the seat and call Val and Evy. Ask them if we can meet tomorrow night. Then I force myself to snap another of life's pieces—one that has been so hard for me to find—into place: acceptance.

God grant me the serenity to accept the things I cannot change and to change the things I can. Bless me with the strength to love and protect three more souls.

Once I accept my future, truly accept what God is asking of me, the image of my puzzle begins to take form, and the mother inside me is reborn.

Chapter Twenty-five - The village

"It's an African proverb." Evy sets a plate with a variety of crackers in front of me and a cheese board with Brie, Gouda, and habanero Cheddar as far away from me as the length of the coffee table will permit.

My stomach agitates. I turn my back, but because there isn't a crumb of food remaining inside me, I only dry heave.

Everyone "Ewwws."

"Sorry," I apologize.

Evy quickly moves the cheese board to a side table and sticks a vase of flowers in front of it, to stifle the smell.

Bennett cringes. "I'm glad I'm a guy." He thinks for a moment then adds, "A gay guy."

"Not fair," Val sings. "You've never been pregnant nor lived with anyone pregnant, yet you reap the benefits of two nieces and two stepdaughters. You ought to have to pay."

"Oh, he'll pay," I say. I haven't made my big announcement. I expect Bennett's life is about to change like mine. I'm going to ask him for help.

I prefaced our little meeting with a spiel to Evy, admitting over the phone I can't raise another child alone. I carefully designed my sentence with a singular noun.

"What African proverb?" I dip the edge of a napkin in a glass filled with water and dab the back of my neck.

Evy winces.

"What? I'm hot."

He shakes his head, then leans back in a white slipcovered chair and sips wine, a king in his castle, his minimalistic nature mirrored around him. No clutter. No television. Pure white furniture with few adornments.

We spread ourselves across his sunroom, ten tall windows, no blinds or curtains, showcasing the spark of his fenced-in back yard. A large solar lantern shines in the middle of a patch of smartly trimmed grass, accent lights glow from behind plant leaves along the fence, and a string of taut, straight lights dangle along the brim of his porch, drawing the beauty of the twinkling dusk inside.

Four soft corners of the sunroom box us in with simple, yet bright-colored vases of fresh flowers plucked from his garden. I slip my shoes onto the white Persian rug that protects Evy's hardwood floor, settle back into my comfy seat, and tuck my bare feet beneath me, feeling my decision to call the troops to Evy's house, perfect.

If I can't be in my house, which is crowded with kids right now, there's no other place I'd rather be than Evy's. Well, other than my best friend's, Jody's, that is, which exists halfway across the country. But Evy's warm and simple home is the perfect atmosphere to tell my friends that my life is about to change.

That I am determined to change.

"It's an old saying. You've heard it." Evy swirls a hand in the air. "'It takes a village to raise a child.' Hilary Clinton used it for a book title."

"Yes, I've read it."

"You. Read Hilary Clinton's book." Evy's neck snaps back like a chicken's. "Oh, c'mon."

"All right, the picture book. I read the picture book. Are you happy? I'm not big on politics. I'm more of a *Yes Please* reader."

"Amy Poehler?" Evy acts appalled but then tucks a hand under his chin. "I love that girl."

"What am I? At book club?" Val hates to read.

"No." I sip then set my Coke on a coaster. "I've come to the conclusion I need a plan in place before I have…to give birth."

"Yes, you do." Evy lifts his wine, moves his wrist in a circle, and the little legs wave up and down.

I gag.

"For heaven's sake. Stop watching my tears."

"Your what?"

"Tears. Legs." He grows frustrated at my ignorance. "My wine. Stop watching me swirl it."

"Motion makes me sick."

He sets it down. "Coffee disgusts you. Cheese constipates you. Wine sickens you. When are you due? I'm not sure how much longer I can take your gagging. Did the doctor say why you are still sick?"

"Oh, yes. Yes, she did."

"Fess up," Val says. "I presume everything is okay. You're pallid but not crying."

This, I deserve. Crying foreshadows most of my serious conversations. "That depends on your definition of okay."

As I say this, clouds must zip past the top of Evy's house and disappear from the evening sky, because light cascades onto his back yard and peeks into the sunroom as if a miracle is about to materialize right on Evy's lawn. We all turn and see a waterfall of rays flowing from a full moon.

"That was weird," Val says.

"Very," Bennett agrees.

Evy slowly swings his gaze toward me as if he's had some paranormal epiphany. Then he floors me by saying, "I know why you called us here. You need our help. You're having twins, aren't you?"

The room holds its breath while I decide how to proceed.

"Nope," I respond.

"Thank God," he lifts his wine and sips. "Now that would be catastrophic."

They all chuckle, agree, and I allow them their fun because I am about to ask them to help me for the next year or two or ten. I sit quietly, drinking my Coke while they joke and enjoy their wine at my expense.

Then I swing and smack them with my club. "Triplets."

A silence separates me from them as if it's the middle of the night, the entire world is sleeping, and one tiny squeak might wake the monster in the room.

They gaze at me, each other, then Bennett and Val burst into hysterics, and Evy frowns.

"Now that would be funny," Bennett manages to say once his laughter subsides.

"Hilarious. That would be hilarious," Val adds. She gulps down wine. "Can you imagine?"

I stare Evy straight in the eyes. He glares back, trying to read me. "It would be a medical miracle," he says.

I squeeze my face into a cringe, flash a smile, then nod. "Yes, it would be. A forty-seven-year-old, no fertility drugs, unmarried—how did Gianna put it?—knocked up, pregnant with triplets. Yes, Evy, that would be a medical miracle."

Evy stands so fast his red wine sloshes over the sides of his glass onto his white carpet. "Oh. My. God."

Bennett, who cares little for scrapes and spills, hops down on his knees and dabs the red wine out of the carpet because Evy will be a bear later if he realizes his posh rug is ruined. "Evy, what's wrong with you? You spilled—" He stops patting.

Slowly, he bends a knee and sets a foot on the ground. He heaves himself upward.

Val jumps up. "You're not—not really?"

I nod. "Oh, yes I am. I'm a freakin' medical miracle."

"Triplets?" Her voice cracks in the middle of the word.

"Yep."

"That's impossible."

"Well, now I'm disappointed in you, Val. You've underestimated me."

Their faces sag and mouths gape. They bounce glances toward one another, their eyes begging someone to tell them this horrific fact isn't true. I wait for their shock to subside. I'm not sure my shock has subsided yet, so I give them the time they need to digest my current situation.

They stand dazed for a full minute, maybe two, then they react. However, not how I expect. I expect concern. Surprise. Compassion. Perhaps denial but, at least, sympathy. Instead, I receive unbridled laughter—even Evy, the laugh-control master who camouflages merriment like a pro, can't squash a chuckle.

He releases a few sighs in between chortles, clicking his tongue and shaking his head disapprovingly as if this is something I can change. Bennett, stretched out on the ground, gasps for air breathlessly, and Val repeats "I can't believe it," over and over like a broken old victrola.

When they gather themselves, Evy speaks first. "I have said this countless times. Every time I believe you can't surprise me more, you do. This, I trust, you won't be able to top for quite a long time."

"Like forever," Val says. "Are you sure?"

"Sonogram. Three heartbeats."

She covers her mouth with a hand.

"Have you told the kids?" Evy asks.

"No, Blake and I found out late yesterday. I've taken this time to digest the news myself."

"What did Blake say?"

"Nothing."

"He said nothing?"

"It's hard to speak when you're unconscious. I had to rush him to the emergency room because he hit his head on the corner of the examination table during his trek to the floor. Fourteen stitches."

"Now I know you're lying." Bennett steps toward me. "My brother never gets rattled. There's no way he passed out."

"Oh, but he did. The doctor and two nurses scrambled to his side, fighting over the smelling salts to wake him while I sat hyperventilating. He came to while they jockeyed for position."

"I have one simple request, darling, let me be there when you tell Delanie."

"And Gianna," Val adds a request to Evy's. "I can't wait to see her reaction."

"I'm not telling them."

"Well, of course, you are, Naggy. They're your children. You have to tell them."

"Nope." I'm pretty firm with my decision. "Not telling them."

"Nikki." Now Bennett tries to bend my determination. "You have to tell them."

"No, you're wrong. I'm not telling them."

"Then who? If not you, who, Naggy?"

"Their Uncle Evy and Uncle Bennett."

An hour later we—Evy, Bennett, Val, and I, with Leah and Penelope in tow—show up at my house. Bennett drives Leah and Penelope to my friend Ellie's for a few hours. We send my children's friends home (they've invited a ton over because they assumed mom was gone for the evening), and we sit down with Delanie, Hux, and Gianna, and Evy gently relays the news of the triplets.

Long past midnight, after the shouting and screaming and laughing and crying, Val leaves for home, Ellie drops Evy's girls off, and Evy, Bennett, Leah, Penny, Delanie, Hux, Gianna, and I push back the couches and tables in my family room, spread blankets and pillows on the floor, pass out heaping bowls of ice cream, and have the best sleepover of our lives.

We burn two campfire-scented candles at either end of the room, turn out the lights in the entire house, draw the shades, and plug in twinkle lights, stringing them from one corner of the ceiling to another. Then we lie down on our backs and gaze up at our makeshift stars, talking about dreams and love and the true meaning of life—oh, and who will or won't change poopy diapers.

I stay awake after everyone else is asleep, devouring their quiet, beautiful faces, cherishing this moment in time. A love, somewhere deep inside my soul, shimmies up my spine. I close my heavy eyelids, and the same peace I experienced the prior night encompasses me. I'm not sure how this acceptance has come over me.

I pray silently that the calmness enveloping me surrounds Blake, too. I'm not sure men, who never experience life growing inside them, can truly love a child more than themselves. Besides these kids, Blake has a budding career and fame to master, and the delight of fame is hard to contain even for those who swore they never wanted it. The higher the peak you summit, the harder the descent.

I pray Blake comes to terms with having three more children.

I glance around the room one last time before closing my eyes. Each of us will likely attempt to recreate this family-room campout many times throughout the remainder of our lives, but until our dying days, what we've built here tonight will never be refashioned—and never be undone.

Tonight, a village was born.

Chapter Twenty-six - The Rueda

Throughout Friday and Saturday, the media had marveled over and guessed about the black-stitched scar on the left side of Blake's forehead, but to my knowledge, Blake told no one how he'd hurt himself.

He didn't call on Saturday night as promised.

I pray he wants to be a part of our village.

Before his first round of golf early Sunday morning, he sent a text apologizing, saying he was exhausted and hoped to stay in Canada after his final round to get a good night's sleep. He asked if I was okay if he caught a plane home Monday morning. He could be back in Erie early afternoon.

Of course, I said yes. Recently experiencing my epiphany, promising to remain calm and not sweat the trivial annoyances that creep into life because now my entire world is about to change, I tamped down my insecurity and tried not to personalize Blake's change in plans.

Right away I realize changing my inherent hypersensitivity won't be easy. A gurgle of worry wails from my belly. Then I remember three beings, who will be engulfed by their own set of problems, live inside me. I say a prayer and tell myself I—we—will be all right.

On Sunday morning when Bennett wakes, sleepy-eyed and swathed in blankets on my family-room floor, I read Blake's text to him. He rests his head on a pillow, wipes his eyes, then whispers he's worried about his brother. First, because Blake has never passed out in his life, and second, because he needs an extra day due to exhaustion. Typically, he's full of energy and overly grounded.

"Maybe he's not sleeping well." I sit up and fold my legs beneath me.

"He's a sound sleeper." Bennett sits up, too. "Other than his divorce, he holds his emotions in check no matter what life throws his way." His gaze darts to me. He must realize this might upset me. He reaches a hand over Evy, who sleeps between us, and squeezes my hand. "But please don't worry. He loves you. He just needs time to digest this."

Right then, a picture flashes on the television screen. We've left it on all night. The bright flicker catches our attention. It's a sports channel. Golf. Bennett reaches for the remote and turns the sound up enough for the two of us to hear.

"The mystery man has been identified," a newscaster announces, and a picture of two people, one being me, fills every inch of the screen. I hardly recognize myself I'm so big. The other person, a guy, is dark-haired, blue-eyed, and gorgeous. I have my hand on his shoulder.

"What the heck?" I wiggle, lean forward, and study the man.

The newscast switches back to the newsroom. Two newscasters flank a screen with a smaller version of the picture in between them. "Larry's quite the looker," one says.

OMG.

That's not Lawrence. At least it isn't Lawrence Looney. It's Peter. Lawrence Peter, the thirty-year-old accountant who is drop-dead gorgeous. The sports show has dug up a Christmas photo from last year's office party.

Agnese.

In the photo, I'm standing behind Peter, squeezing his shoulder, smiling. He's gazing at me, fondly, admiringly.

Bennett barks out his surprise, "That's Larry?"

I rub my eyes as if I might wipe Peter away.

"No, no, no. That's Lawrence Peter."

Evy hears me and props his head up, shoving his eye mask onto his forehead so he can see. "What's happening that you disturb my beauty sleep?"

Bennett extends an arm and points. "They're talking about Nikki and Larry on TV."

Evy studies the screen. "Well, that's Naggy, but that's not Larry."

"It's a different Larry," I say. "Larry Peter."

"Who?"

I shoot a brief explanation Bennett's way. "A kid in my office who goes by his middle name. They think I'm carrying on with him, Lawrence Peter."

"My, my." Evy rises, clumsily squirms into a sitting position. "He certainly doesn't have Larry hair."

"That's because he's twenty-six," I shout.

"Is this the stud daddy?" We've woken Hux.

"No!" I'm appalled.

"Who's Peter?" Bennett turns the volume up, and the newscaster's voice bellows across my family room, "And the Blake Anderson saga continues..."

"Stop that, can you, Bennett?"

He freezes the frame. Someone's photoshopped a different dress on me, lowered the front, shortened the hem. The dress I wore that year was green, not red.

"That's not my body.

Rutger.

She's airbrushed the people around us out of the photo, too. I remember that party distinctly. Sherry was beside me. I'd just told Peter I thought the temp girl working for us at the time had a crush on him. Being the mother of two girls, I warned him to be kind to her. "Don't hurt this one. She's too sweet," I'd said. If I remember correctly, he quipped, "Thanks, Mom."

This picture tells a different story.

"That's not my dress," I say. "They've painted one on me. I look like a floozy."

Evy leans away. "It's not like you've never worn a low-cut dress before."

"To an office Christmas party? With half my chest showing? Never."

"She's not that voluptuous." Delanie has awoken. "At least she wasn't before she got herself pregnant."

My gaze falls to my chest and back to the TV. Have they photoshopped a current picture of me in? Can't be.

"You're busting out of that dress, Aunt Nikki," Penny sits up.

Something about family time centering around your boobs is so wrong.

"I don't own a dress like that. I swear."

"Do they mention the triplets?" Delanie asks.

Bennett hits play and we listen to an entire clip about Blake Anderson barely making the Sunday finals. He captured the last spot.

I'm not sure what that means but Bennett remarks, "I'm sure he's upset over finishing low."

"Not as upset as he'll be if they mention the triplets," I say.

They flash a second picture next to mine. It's Lawrence Peter. At the beach. He's topless, his stomach ripped with muscle.

"Oh. My. Goodness," Evy remarks.

"Stop staring at him," I scold.

"Yeah, Uncle Evy. We like Bennett." I'm not sure how long Gianna has been watching but she's wide-eyed. "We're keeping him."

"Thank you, Gianna." Bennett holds up a hand, and Gianna high fives him.

"Don't get all bent of shape. Can't a man look?" Evy kicks his blanket aside.

Somehow, even when my face is perched on the screen and announcers suggest I'm having relations with a twenty-something boy, who is pictured half-naked on the beach, my family manages to turn the conversation away from me.

"He's twenty-eight." Delanie corrects my age estimate of Peter.

"Who?" Gianna leans toward her sister.

"Larry. Peter. Whatever his name is. Facebook says he's twenty-eight."

"Dad, what are those lines on his stomach?" Leah asks.

"Those are what you call spectacular abs," Evy answers.

"Lists him as in a relationship but there are no pictures of any girls." Delanie scrolls through Peter's profile.

"How did you find that so fast?" I gaze over her shoulder.

"His picture is all over the internet. It says Nikki, 47, dating Larry, 28."

Briefly, I wonder if this is the reason Blake hasn't called.

"Mom, the cradle robber," Hux says.

"I am not a cradle robber. He dates some girl. Although now that I think about it, I'm pretty sure she's married."

"Mom, come clean. It's you, isn't it?" Hux, again.

I lean and smack him on the shoulder. "No, not me. I don't know who she is. I'm not even sure it's true. That's the office rumor."

"Then why are you so chummy with him?" Gianna asks.

"I wasn't being chummy." My gosh, even my kids think I'm a floozy. "I was chastising him for flirting with a temp. Agnese snapped this picture."

"Were you jealous?"

I smack Hux again. "Stop."

He laughs. "Mom, we know you and this guy aren't doing the dirty deed. You think guys like him like old ladies?"

Honestly, there's no end to the rudeness of my children.

"Did you say, Aggie?" Evy's referring to the picture taker.

"Yes. And somebody—probably Rutger—photoshopped it because that's not my dress. I'm going to kill her."

"Upwards of sixty percent of women in prison are mothers, so you'll be in good company." Evy annoyingly relays incarceration facts. "And half suffer mental health issues, so you'll be doubly at home."

"Shut up, Evy."

"Don't you mean be quiet?" Hux reminds me of my house rules of grammar.

"I mean be quiet. This isn't funny."

"Naggy, last night you promised to remain calm. Not jump to conclusions. Smell the roses. All that," Evy reminds me.

"Turn the sound up, Bennett." I ignore him.

Bennett hits play and we listen to the newscaster disparage a relationship I'm not having with someone twenty years younger than me. They mention Mark, my ex, and Blake's ex-wife. Then, when the picture changes, I think they've moved on to another story.

I look away, stand, and gather up strewn blankets to fold, but I hear Blake's name once again, glance up, and lo and behold, a picture tempts my new-found convictions.

"Freeze that," I yell.

Bennett's quick finger captures the frame and everyone moves closer to the television set. A million pixels of color assemble on my fifty-five-inch screen and capture the perfect image of Blake sitting next to Rutger Rosy at a dimly lit table for two in an upscale Canadian restaurant. A Canadian flag stretches alongside the wall behind them. His hand is perched on the back of her chair. Their faces, wide and somber, seem engaged in some secret conversation.

"Okay, this can't be good," Hux mumbles.

"Naggy." Evy stands and places himself between me and the television screen.

"Move out of the way, Evy."

"Remember. No jumping to conclusions."

"Get your skinny ass out of the way." I squirm onto my knees and shove him. "He's with Rosy."

"There has to be some explanation." Bennett stands, his eyes searching the floor. "Where's my phone?"

"It's after seven. He's already golfing." Hux stands and everyone follows suit.

There, amidst a mound of covers and pillows, we listen to two announcers laugh about Blake and me, the hot Larry, the beautiful Rosy, and I wonder if they understand how their catty quips cut.

The announcer laughs. "Isn't that Rosy Parker, David Thompson's ex-fiancée? Looks like there's some Salsa Rueda going on in the golf world."

Chapter Twenty-seven - The pleas

I've been emotionally crippled for most of my life, allowing the way other people perceive me to dictate how I view myself. Changing that pattern will be hard, but I'll begin by not allowing my children to coerce me back into my old ways.

Of course, they blame me for the media muddle confusing Peter with Lawrence, and I agree my initial lie about Lena being pregnant may have triggered this entire confusing mess, but I'm not the only culprit. Someone provided pictures of Peter to the press and lied about our relationship.

Still, children blame their mothers for the smallest of snags in life, so this is no different. They like Blake and worry I've pushed him away. If I wasn't so insecure, they argued; if I wasn't always sticking my nose in other people's business; if I hadn't gotten pregnant; if I wasn't selfishly thinking of myself all the time, and blah, blah, blah they point out every idiosyncrasy I have ever had and remind me of every mistake I've made, back to in utero. If I hadn't done all of these horrendously foolish things, Blake wouldn't have taken Rutger Rosy to dinner.

Seriously? You spoiled, spoiled brats.

On Sunday night, Blake finally texts me:

I can explain everything.

I don't respond. I'm not sure if I'm more upset with him for dining with Rosy or with my kids for pointing their fingers at me all day long and accusing me of chasing Blake away.

He texts more:

Bennett explained about Peter…not being Lawrence.

I resist the temptation to type: Are you at dinner with Rosy? Choke on cheese.

I don't want to be a woman who jumps to conclusions, but I also don't want to be a woman marrying a man who jumps into bed with another woman at the first signs of hardship. How did his first marriage really end?

After a minute, three little dots surface on my cell. I wait. Another text appears:

He said ur upset....please...not what it seems...will explain tomorrow.

Finally, I break down and text him. Though I want to remain loyal to my pledge of being patient, kind, understanding, and not sweating the small moments in life (is this small?), I'm tempted to tap obscenities into the phone about where he and Rutger Rosy can go. The letters I tap form words somewhere in between the two thoughts:

Nope. Not upset. Busy, sick, tired. Find a ride home tomorrow.

He responds:

Nikki...please.

I hold firm:

I work tomorrow. Text Bennett for a ride.

I plug my charger into a kitchen socket. My cell pings, but I resist the urge to read any more texts. I place my phone on its charger and walk away, hurrying up the stairs, so I can't hear the dings.

I lie awake for hours, tossing and turning, reminding myself that I have three dependent embryos swimming inside me, relying on me to hold myself together.

A little after 3 AM when I'm about to break down into a horrific sob, a sudden tingling sensation strikes me—in more than one spot. Not one, or two, but three strong twinges in three separate areas of my stomach.

Life. A miracle in so many ways.

It's God. I'm sure. He's showering me with strength and fortifying my conviction. Hinting that I must learn to cope with whatever life sends me. Not only for myself but for my children.

The woman inside me rises.

With or without Blake Anderson, we'll be all right.

Chapter Twenty-eight - The decision

The office buzzes with chatter. When I walk in fifteen minutes late, everyone stops talking and silence ushers me to my cubicle. I drop my purse at my desk and head toward Jack Bruno's office.

"Nikki." With a sympathetic drawl to my name, Lawrence Peter catches my attention. He's followed me into the hallway.

I hold up a hand. "I'm sorry you were dragged into the middle of my life drama."

In my peripheral vision, I catch the outline of Agnese in the entryway. She quickly and sheepishly ducks inside the receptionist's office. Peter and I share a glance and a frown, then I continue on my way. Larry catches up to me, reaches for my hand, and tucks a heart-shaped key chain inside my fingers. I glance down. The words "Be strong" shimmer in gold from the palm of my hand.

"It's from Lena," he tells me.

I wrap my arms around him, no longer caring what anyone thinks, then I head up the stairs to find Jack.

I spill everything about the weekend to him, gently alluding to my big news, and right when I am about to tell him that I am pregnant with triplets, there is a knock on the door and Lawrence enters without being asked in.

"This is personal, Larry," Jack lets him know.

"No," I say. "I have something else to tell you, Jack, and I want Lawrence to hear this, too. So if you don't mind, is it okay if he stays?"

Jack waves him in, and Lawrence closes the door behind him.

As soon as Lawrence takes a seat beside me, I tactlessly blurt out the news. "I'm pregnant with triplets."

Neither Jack nor Lawrence knows how to react. Their eyes glaze over, and I can read the questions in their vacant stares. Triplets? What's the appropriate, politically correct response? How should I react? Are congratulations in order?

Finally, Lawrence places his palm on the top of my hand and squeezes. "It will be okay, Nikki."

I wipe tears away. "Yes, it will. But I'm sure we can agree that I can't be Bruno's CFO, and that's the reason I wanted Lawrence present. I want to recommend him for the position. He's hard-working, loyal, and has highly underestimated himself for years. He can do this job, Jack."

What happens next in the quiet of a great boss's office is the three of us work magic. Larry agrees that, with a little help, he can handle the job. Then he proceeds to say he will have to hire a competent full-time or part-time assistant once Jerry Conway is gone, and he makes the case why hiring an experienced part-time worker would be so much more beneficial than training a new full-timer. I hardly say anything. Lawrence convinces both Jack and me that I could work from home one or two days a week and spend a few hours in the office when Blake is home.

"The two of us love this business, Jack. If we can't handle the job together, we will step down, but at least let us try," he says.

I remind him I'll have my hands full. I may not be able to work at all.

"Lena can help," he replies. "We wanted to make an offer to you and Blake. Now more than ever, I believe it is appropriate. With everything that has gone on in your life lately, Lena didn't want to bother you, but she lost her job. Her company folded. She said if you'll let her, she'd love to watch the baby for you a few days a week."

"Babies," I correct.

He smiles. "She can handle them. Lena is quite a woman."

His words relay comfort both because Lena, someone I trust, wants to help me, and because I was correct about Lawrence. He loves her.

Yet, my head is spinning.

"Thank you for the offer, Lawrence. Everything is fairly fresh in my mind right now, but I suppose, along with all of the help from friends, I'll need to hire a nanny. I'm not sure about working, though."

Let the pieces fall into place, Nikki.

My mother's words forever slip into my thoughts.

"Don't make a decision now. Think about it," he adds.

"I will. You'll have to explain to Lena I'm having triplets, but if her offer to help still stands, I'd love to hire her as our nanny."

Accepting help has never been easy for me—even paid help. I hired a cleaning lady years ago but found myself cleaning for her. Like most mothers, I hate inconveniencing anyone. I'd rather work myself into exhaustion.

"She won't mind more than one baby. Trust me." For the first time in many months, Lawrence appears happy.

A few days ago, Lena called and thanked me for the counselor recommendation. She and Lawrence have been seeing Tracy, who encouraged them to find a common interest. They began singing at a small tavern in their neighborhood on the weekends, with much success. Lena admitted she hasn't been this happy in years.

"She's a wonderful mother," Larry adds (he doesn't mind being called Larry any longer).

He blathers on and after a brief debate, I agree to consider the part-time work offer if we can do a trial run, and as soon as I say this, Lawrence and Jack seem invigorated.

We spend the next hour discussing specifics. Lawrence draws up a plan, and Jack becomes so enthusiastic that I begin to believe maybe I can work a few hours a week. In the end, the three of us stand and shake hands. I'm convinced working is at least a possibility. Jack says there won't be a complicated job description drawn up. If this does come to be, there'll be no contracts, lawyers, human resource personnel, just a handshake and a promise among three good-hearted people to try. Jack and Lawrence are good for their words. They'll let me decide when or if I must leave.

Chapter Twenty-nine - The fingerprints

Later that morning, the fatigue hits me. Whether the meeting with Jack and Lawrence or Blake's impending return wears me down, I'm not sure. After Lawrence presented his plan for me to work part-time, a false sense of invigoration had hit me, and I spent a fast-paced morning juggling balance sheets.

By noon, however, I'd been to the bathroom throwing up three times, once so violently that tiny blood vessels emerged on my cheeks. I applied cool compresses to both sides of my face, but the spider veins remained. Twice, Sherry stopped by and placed her hand on my forehead to check if I was feverish.

Around a quarter after twelve, Jack Bruno steps into my cubicle and orders me to go home.

Behind him, Sherry leans in the doorway. "Nikki, you look terrible. Go home and get some sleep. I'll finish up for you."

"Take this afternoon off and rest. You'll feel better in the morning," Jack adds.

Though I doubt I'll be able to sleep, I can't fight them both. My head is pounding from the vomiting, so I comply. I finish one worksheet, hand the others to Sherry, lock my desk, and head home, hoping this headache is the result of my lack of sleep and not something worse.

Please, don't let anything happen to my babies, Lord.

Once I'm home, I head to the closest place I can lie down, my family room couch. I drop my keys on the coffee table, plunk my purse on the floor, and despite the thoughts racing through my mind, I fall into a much-needed sleep.

I don't hear Blake let himself in. I'm not sure how long he's been there when my eyes flicker open, but I glance toward the time of day beneath my thermostat, and the blue lights display 2:39. I've been sleeping for two hours. Blake's sitting on the edge of the couch, one hand resting on my hip.

Slowly, my vision clears and my gaze focuses on his handsome features: warm brown eyes, perfect lips, a shadow of bristle on chin and cheeks. He's so handsome my breath catches in my throat.

I hate how in love with him I am.

"Hi," he mutters, faintly, apologetically.

"I didn't hear you come in." I attempt to sit up but, gently, he nudges my head back onto the pillow.

"Don't get up. Rest. You look beautiful." He sets the back of one hand against my forehead. "You don't feel warm. I called the office. Sherry said you were flushed. They sent you home."

"I didn't sleep well last night."

He strokes my damp, sweaty hair as if it is satiny soft. "I could sit here all day staring at you." He takes a long breath and expels it forcefully. His eyes dance over my face. "I made a mistake."

For a moment, the old Nikki returns, and my imagination races away. I picture him with Rosy, cuddled in her arms. I edge away from him on the couch and close my eyes. Try to blacken the image. I can't bear it if he slept with her.

"Rosy?" I ask.

"No." He perks up, surprised. "I did go to dinner with her, but no, she and David are getting back together. That's what I wanted to explain. She's not as bad a person as I once thought."

I push myself up on the couch. I may have promised myself I won't jump to conclusions, but I also refuse to be walked on. "Blake, those pictures of me plastered all over the television?"

"I know—"

"No, you don't. Rosy gave them to the media."

"She did. She confessed everything. Said that young guy was not your friend Larry."

"Lawrence," I interrupt.

"Lawrence."

"Was that before or after you took her to dinner?"

"Nikki, you don't understand—"

For some reason, these four words infuriate me. I control my anger as much as possible.

"Blake, she made us look like we were in the middle of some lascivious love triangle. You expect me to believe she's going back to David? You said it yourself; she's a golf groupie. So I need to know. Did you, at the first sign of hardship, trot off with her? I don't understand how you could take her to dinner let alone—"

I stop myself. It occurs to me I might be confusing Mark's tendencies with Blake's. Do I really think he had an affair?

"Nikki," he says softly. "You can't think—"

"I'm sorry. I don't want to make assumptions. I want—I don't know what I want, Blake. I only know I have to hold myself together for these babies."

He slips an arm around my shoulder. "I'm sorry, but not about Rosy. Nothing happened with Rosy. What I'm sorry for and what I can't believe I did was leave you alone when you needed me most." He releases his grip and his eyes meet mine, sincerity tangling with remorse. "I'm sorry for getting on that plane to Canada and leaving you to deal with this. I was in shock. It didn't hit me until I was on the fourth hole of my first round at the tournament, what a mistake I had made."

"Blake, your leaving was not a mistake."

"Yes, it was."

"No, I needed time, too. We both needed time to grasp how our lives are about to change. But I became so confused when you showed up with Rosy at that restaurant on TV. I didn't want to believe you would do anything, but then my mind began spinning."

"Listen to me. I would never cheat on you. I love you." His voice cracks. "But I was wrong. I got on that plane last Thursday and I shouldn't have. On Friday I was in shock, but by Saturday all I could think about was what was I doing there? Why wasn't

I at home with you? I swore to myself I would never leave you when you needed me ever again."

He releases me, and I gaze into his rheumy brown eyes.

"You had a tournament. It's your profession. You had to go. Leaving isn't the problem. You'll have to leave me often. The problem is when you do walk out that door, when I'm left behind with three crying babies and a world jam-packed with turmoil, will I be able to trust that you won't let me down? That you'll love me no matter what? Always come home? I've gone through a divorce once. I never want to again."

"Since the day I met you, I have never wanted any other woman. I believe everything I went through in life, with my ex, my daughters, the roller coaster ride of this golfing career, everything led me to this moment—to you." He sets a palm on my stomach. "To them."

Reflexively, my hand covers his.

"All this time," he continues. "The unrest I felt, wondering what I was doing and where I was going. Those questions disappeared when I met you. I would never cheat. Ever. And I will always come home."

I fold into his warm arms. "And I would never cheat on you, Blake. But I'm angry that you would associate with a woman who tried to sabotage us. Even if David is a nice guy."

"Here's the thing." He inches away so he can look into my eyes. He takes my hands into his. "Sometimes people who are miserable make mistakes they wouldn't have if their life had taken a different turn."

"It sounds as if you're defending her."

"Just listen," he says. "I never paid much attention to Rosy, but I do know David. He's a great guy. When they broke up, I thought, good for him; he doesn't need a girl like that. I'd heard so much about her. Then she approached me after my round on Saturday, crying. She said she had done something awful. To you. She needed to talk to me."

"So you took her to dinner?"

"Sh, listen."

My blood begins racing through my veins. Blake is much more forgiving than me. I want to change. Truly I do. But I'm not a big enough person to forgive Rosy for slipping Agnese's pictures to the press then crying remorsefully.

"Do you know why they broke up?"

"I really don't care why."

"She and David lost a baby."

I snap my head back. "What?" Fear rushes through me and I quiet.

"That's why David has been playing so badly. That's why they broke up and why, when she found out you and I were having a baby, she did something unthinkable."

He draws me close, leans back on the couch, and tucks his chin on the top of my head.

"Honestly, I think God sent her to me Saturday night. Because when she explained she had lost a baby, I panicked. I wanted to catch the next flight home. But David came in and jumped to the conclusion we were on a date. I spent an hour with the two of them. He honestly loves her."

"I believe you. I do. And I don't want to sound mean. But why then didn't you call afterward on Saturday or come home Sunday night?"

"I didn't want to call at one in the morning. I was six hours away from the finals when the two of them finally settled down, and I went to my room. Then, after the match." He stops and frowns. "I bombed; you know."

"I heard," I say, not caring. Regardless of my changed conviction, I'll never be a fan of golf. "Why didn't you just come home?"

"Because they wanted to come with me."

"What?"

"Rosy and David. They are outside in a car. They've been sitting there." He glimpses his watch. "For an hour and ten minutes."

I straighten. "You brought Rutger Rosy here? To my house?"

He nods.

"And David? They're outside?"

Again, a nod.

"What could she want to see me for?"

"She wants to apologize. For everything."

I stand so quickly that I knock Blake's water off the coffee table and have to run for rags to sop it up.

When I finish, he asks. "I can send them home, but, Nikki, I think you should hear her out."

I don't answer. I toss the towel in the sink and lean, stiff-shouldered, on the counter, wondering how much more I can take.

"It's up to you," he says. "I'll understand either way."

I saunter toward the living room and open my front door, gaze through the finger-printed glass. I've cleaned hundreds of fingerprints off that storm door in the last month alone and, still, they remain. Now I fold my arms, square my jaw, and peek around them, imagining the laughs Rosy must have had at my expense. She and that woman, Call-me-Cat, probably talked about me for days after I drove the cart into the pond. Not to mention how they celebrated when the media tagged me ForePlay Nik. People still call me that on Twitter.

I don't think I'm big enough to accept her apology.

I cross my arms stiffly and decide I'll see her, but to tell her off, not forgive her. I straighten, prepare for battle.

She sees me, opens the car door, and slithers out sheepishly. She's crying.

"She told me she always wanted kids." Blake talks behind me. I don't turn around. "And all I could think was how lucky I am." I feel his warmth before his chest nudges against my back. He slips his arms around me, setting his fingers on my belly, and kisses my cheek from behind. "Somewhere deep inside me I suddenly felt like the luckiest person in the world. I understood why she is such a nasty person."

"Well, I'm sorry she had a miscarriage, but she was mean before that," I say, but Blake has softened my spite. "Remember the golf tournament?"

"I mentioned that, and she admitted her aunt had been bad-mouthing you for months. Somehow, Agnese overheard Jack talking to his father about offering you that promotion."

"That doesn't surprise me."

"She told Rosy you'd stolen the job from her." His arms tighten around me. "She's sorry, Nik. I think this miscarriage and break up with David made her take a good long look at herself—at her life."

My vision switches from Rosy to the fine lines of the fingerprints on my door. I lean my head back onto Blake's shoulder, sinking into his warmth. I think I hear Gianna moving around upstairs. A zigzagging twinge crosses my belly. Blake's soft breath, in and out, caresses me, and I suddenly feel it, too—my fortune, my luckiness.

Am I big enough to forgive her?

What I've learned about revenge over the years is that it needs an eddy to survive. Saying something hurtful provokes someone else to react spitefully. Their spitefulness stirs the storm, and you respond with more bitter words or hurtful actions, and the cycle continues, swirling, never-ending. The hurt and vengeance may quiet for a while but can flare up, anywhere, anytime. The two souls become trapped in a vortex, grasping for others to help them out but tugging them into the vacuum instead. The bitterness grows. The hurt twists and spirals so long that no one can remember what the original quarrel was about.

I know what stops the whirling. One soul must step out of the circle.

Can I do that? Am I strong—enough?

Rosy plods from the street to my driveway. I inch away from Blake, open the storm door, and step onto my porch. When our eyes meet, the palms of her hands snap upward, covering her face, and she begins sobbing. When we reach each other, stand face-to-face, I can barely understand her, she's crying so hard.

"I'm so sorry, Nikki. I'm such a jealous person. I hate myself for it."

Something clicks inside me. Something enlightening about the female gender and self-judgment.

Women love so fiercely that we personalize the smallest incidents. We hurt easily, and we fight back fiercely without realizing anger doesn't strengthen us. It weakens us. We lash out, wrongly wanting someone else to hurt like us. Then later, when turmoil rises in our soul, we don't understand why we feel sorrow. But that unrest inside us, what torments our soul, is our inability to forgive ourselves for the hurt we've caused others—even when we've apologized and been forgiven.

Women are hardest on themselves. We are often given and accept blame. We pardon others but not ourselves.

Today, I see the sorrow in Rosy. It's clear. Deep down, Rosy detests herself for the pain she's caused me.

Now I have a choice.

Think, Nikki, think before you speak.

She has no children. I will have six of my own. Eight when I count Blake's two girls. What if Blake had no children? What if there was no Delanie or Hux or Gianna or triplet number one or triplet two (okay, oh my gosh!) or triplet three? How alone would I feel?

You're lucky to have those fingerprints, Nikki. Don't let them cloud your vision.

In front of me, two clear options materialize. I can personalize Rosy's anger and hang on to my hurt, or I can stop the maelstrom.

I step forward. Rosy cringes, flinching as if I might slap her. But I wrap my arms around her, and she drops her head onto my shoulder, crying like a child—a tall, lean, slobbery child. I have to rise onto my tiptoes to comfort her because she's so tall.

"I'm so sorry. I'm so sorry," she repeats over and over.

My anger releases, and instead of hating Rutger Rosy, a soft, hidden spot in my heart opens up, and I let her in.

Chapter Thirty - The move

Two months later, the deep green hues outside Blake's picture window fade to shades of orange, red, and yellow. Crisp windswept leaves float by, a tepid breeze blowing off a still-warm Lake Erie rattles the window glass, and v-shaped flocks of birds soar in the distance, warblers, sparrows, and other songbirds flying south because of the days ahead.

Beyond the edge of Blake's yard, blue waves with white crests cavort across the bay. Autumn has arrived, bringing with it all its splendor. No other season can compare to Pennsylvania's fall loveliness.

Gianna and I moved in with Blake halfway through September. Our house went on the market after Gianna announced she would love to change schools. Unbeknownst to me, two of her friends, along with a boy she's had her eye on since middle school, enrolled in a Catholic high school here in Erie. She hadn't dared to ask if she could attend because of the divorce and tuition costs, but when she let it slip that she had wanted to go there all along, Blake insisted on driving her up the following Saturday for a tour. He's friends with the school's golf coach, of course.

While Gianna enrolled, she will not be golfing. Hannah, on the other hand, is down in Wheeling breaking records for her high school. She's inherited Blake's talent. Sophie has, too, though time will tell if her energetic personality can relax enough to play eighteen holes.

They are here this Friday morning in anticipation of our big weekend. Blake picked up Hannah and Sophie yesterday afternoon, and Hux and Delanie arrived last night. We've strategically planned our wedding ceremony for tomorrow, so everyone can be here. Blake's girls are on fall break, and Delanie, a senior in college, has no classes on Friday so she came home last night to help with the preparations. Hux, of course, offered to sacrifice and skip his Friday and Monday classes. We aren't sure how often he attends class, anyway. That boy could slide his way up a ladder. He has a perfect 3.0 at the University of Virginia, his carefree spirit tempered by a high IQ that the good Lord bestowed upon him.

Having all five children at home is a blessing.

"What are you doing?" Delanie steps beside me and glances out the window, wondering what I'm gazing at. I swing an arm around her shoulder. She frowns and wiggles free.

I smile. I love her headstrong ways.

"Nothing," I say. "Just taking in the day."

"Shouldn't you be getting ready? We have manicures scheduled at noon."

Off to one side of Blake's yard, the edges of a large white tent are tied to side posts, and two brawny men carry a heater inside. Behind them, a woman struggles to keep a box of colorful centerpieces in her grasp as the wind picks up.

We've invited forty-eight people to tomorrow's wedding. Lena and Larry will serenade Blake, me, the kids, our closest friends, and a few neighbors, Emma and Giff, who live next door, and Ally and Rhett, who live across the street. These are the neighbors who watch over me when Blake is out of town, golfing.

God brings the people we need into our lives at the exact correct time.

"I will soon." I sip coffee. My nausea has finally subsided. I'm twenty-five weeks along, but people often remark, "Any day now?"

I can't imagine my waistline circumference in three months.

We hear a knock on the door and Evy barges in, holding a dress in the air. "Here you go, Naggy. You owe me. I had it laundered and pressed for you."

Instantly, Delanie barks, "Mom, what's Evy doing with that old dress?"

I indulge in several slurpy sips of coffee before responding, enjoying the moment while I can. "Because the new one doesn't fit."

"The ivory dress? For the wedding? Doesn't fit?"

Delanie drove home three weekends ago when Blake and I decided to forego a large wedding and plan a quiet ceremony in the back yard. She and Gianna helped me choose the perfect, creamy-white wedding dress with satiny fringe and lacey sleeves.

"No, it doesn't." I down the last of my coffee. "I can't zip it."

"And you're not—" She hesitates, studying me. "Having a conniption?"

I turn toward her, ready to reply but, behind her, I see Blake descending the stairs, clean-shaven, wearing holey jeans, and sporting a baseball cap that says "Save the Turtles."

My heart flutters, and I feel the corners of my lips twitch upward. "No, my blue dress is fine," I say.

Blake's face lights up, and he smiles back, wiggling his hat snuggly down his forehead. Wearing the snapback has come to mean "remain calm" as in "don't start swinging." He came across the gem at a Florida tournament and wears it mostly when the kids are at home.

"Are you sure?" Delanie is still scrutinizing me.

"I'm sure."

"And…you're not throwing a tantrum?"

"What good would that do? It's not like the dress will somehow expand and fit me."

Evy steps forward and sets the back of his hand on my forehead.

"Question," he says and I'm certain he's about to ask how I'm feeling. But no, Evy must test my sudden serenity. "Could you not have been this calm last year before my wedding? Maybe then you would have preserved my rings. And my auntie's dress?"

"Evy." Bennett has followed him in.

"Okay, okay, all is forgotten," he says then a twinkle in his eye surfaces and he whispers, "You do know I'm going to drink heavily tomorrow and throw up on someone."

"I expect it." I laugh.

Blake steps beside me, kisses my cheek, and leans toward Evy. "Make sure it's not me. Okay, Ev?" He winks and heads out the back door.

Gianna bounces down the steps, "Do you like my new dress?"

"I love it. You look wonderful, Gianna." I've learned to hold my tongue about my daughters' tastes.

"Do you know where my shoes are?"

"In the front closet."

She hurries to shuffle through a mess on the closet floor, retrieves a pair of heels, and slips them on while Evy heads upstairs with my dress. "They'll sink in the grass," he tells her.

She shrugs. Bennett, Hannah, and Sophie discuss the beauty but impracticality of Gianna's heels on their way out the back door. They've promised to help Blake trim bushes and rake leaves for our big day, so I'm left alone with my two precious daughters.

"Why was Evy taking that dress upstairs?" Gianna sizes me up.

"Because her new one doesn't fit," Delanie answers for me.

"What's wrong with her?" Gianna says. "She's not spazzing out."

"I don't know." Delanie sets her hands on her hips.

"It's only a dress. It doesn't matter which one I wear." I meander toward the window and gaze outside, watching Blake.

He stands in the middle of the yard, directing workers toward a looming white tent with windswept sides. A surge of an October breeze drifting off the bay sends one tent flap fluttering. Blake rushes to secure it, and the men with the chairs and long white tables file in. That task complete, Blake taps the shoulder of another worker and points to the other side of the yard where a makeshift altar bends toward our property line. He motions with both hands for the man to right the tilt. I chuckle, picturing it slowly leaning until it hits the ground right as we declare our vows.

I stare fondly at him as Hux joins his sisters behind me, and the three of them discuss my calmness.

"Yeah," Gianna relays, glad to have the edge on them. "She hasn't yelled in a month."

I continue standing at the window as they whisper. It's true. I don't lose my temper as often. I'm not cured, by any means, of all of my idiosyncrasies, but I'm accepting of my new plate. Happy about three new members being added to our family.

Right then, in the middle of Blake giving instructions, his eyes cross the picture window then spring back to meet mine. He stops mid-sentence. The workers glance confusedly at each other, then hurry away as Blake's face relaxes into a smile, and we stare at each other from a distance.

Here is what I've learned. To love another person, truly love them, you must first accept yourself as you are. I'm not perfect. Blake's not perfect. But we do the best we can every day. I stand on one side of the picture glass, and he stands on the other, he, the famous golf pro, and me, the soon-to-be mother of six, our worlds distinct but forever joined.

Just as Blake advised, the tide did turn, and I had my fifteen minutes of fame. When the news that we were having triplets hit the airwaves, there was a media blitz. Blake and I were everywhere. Our names hit numerous television stations from major networks to cable access channels. Savannah Guthrie (my idol) called to chat. Kelly Ripa requested an interview. So many famous people sent photographers to the curb of our home that we often had to pull into our neighbor's driveway and sneak across our lawn to get inside.

Seems being an internet sensation is not all I thought it was.

When the crowd died down and the photographers went home—football and its accompanying myriad of player troubles had begun—I was forgotten.

And it did not hurt.

I realized the quiet lives in this world matter as much as the loud ones. Blake and I are different in many ways. People follow him around, snap photos of him, ask for autographs, and, no different than Rosy, he gives them what they want. But he'd rather be at home with me and the kids.

And me? I had always envied those people with clear-cut paths in life. Those like Blake, who never doubted what they were meant to do. I especially envied souls who found fame— even more so than fortune. What seems like centuries ago, Hux had accused me of wanting to be an "internet sensation." I responded with a "yes, maybe I did."

That was a hard lesson to learn.

Blake is grounded and content, and I'm nervous and always wanting more, but we are alike in that we are honest, loyal, and totally and utterly in love with each other. Cliché as it sounds, we were and are and always will be soulmates. Two very different people combining gifts, goodness, faults, and families. His calmness has rubbed off on me, and I'd like to think my zest for life has inspired him.

Through the clear glass, he winks and tosses me a kiss amidst the complete backyard chaos. I lift both hands to my lips and toss one back.

Then it happens.

While every person can control how they react to adverse effects in life, not a single one of us can control fate. There as I stand gazing lovingly at the man I am about to marry, fate swoops down and sends my calmness running. A tightness shoots across my stomach and settles mercilessly in my back. I latch a hand onto the windowsill while fright overpowers me, sending me to my knees. I wait for the pain to pass.

I've been in labor three times in my life, and I'm fairly certain this is the real deal.

This is too early.

Outside, Blake sees I've fallen to the floor. His smile fades and he dashes toward the house. Evy appears beside me, and my kids gather around. The squeezing stops, then comes back a second and third time while people help me up and rush around me, tapping in telephone numbers, grabbing clothes and keys and cells.

Evy and Bennett lead me out the front door while Blake backs the car out of the garage. Delanie helps me in, tosses a bag in the back seat, and leans into the passenger seat.

"Everything will be all right, Mom." She hugs me softly, and a chill rises within me when the warmth of her embrace leaves me. She closes my door, and my gaze meets Gianna's. I roll down my window to see her clearly.

Standing on the front porch beside Blake's girls, Gianna sets the palms of both hands over her heart as if she loves me then raises them to her lips. She looks young, frightened. Sophie is holding her in her arms, and Hannah strokes her back. I holler to her not to cry that I'll be fine.

The last thing I see and feel as Blake backs out of the driveway and heads toward the hospital, are Gianna's fingers thrusting forward, and a soft breeze brushing my cheek as if her good-luck kiss has found me.

But I know I'm only twenty-five weeks along.

Please Fate, be merciful.

Chapter Thirty-one - The couch

Blake rushes me to the hospital on that gusty October day. He drives fast, as if his life depends on this one drive. He maneuvers in and out of neighborhoods, slicing the wind, skipping stops, rolling through red lights. I barely have time to pray a full rosary. My thoughts wander, catch on those dark crevices of old, conjure disastrous outcomes, and I must willfully force myself back to prayer, faith.

I will not lose these children.

We arrive and an orderly rushes me down a separate corridor reserved for problem pregnancies in the labor and delivery ward. A nurse hooks me to a monitor and examines my cervix, determining it has thinned but hasn't dilated. The doctor pays a visit, a needle is plunged into my arm, and the drip, drip, drip of some fluid concoction slithers down a clear tube and disappears into my body.

After several hours, which seem like an entire gestational period, the squeezing stops, a sonogram is performed—three hearts still beat inside me—and the doctor goes home. Blake falls asleep in a chair beside me. He sleeps fitfully throughout the night, leaning his head on the bedrail, then my pillow, then the crook of his arm. He clutches my hand fiercely, holding so tightly that I must wiggle my fingers every so often to ease the numbness.

He never lets go.

In the morning, Doctor Yank returns with the results of the sonogram—two girls, one boy, which seems so unimportant now. She relays all the tests taken and blood drawn are normal, including my blood levels from the epilepsy medication. Blake and I take much-needed long, relaxing breaths.

Despite my pristine health and halted contractions, she is sending me home on a confined-activity condition. She admits she expected such an episode because of my age. The mere fact I'm carrying triplets is a miracle in itself, she remarks. She orders me to complete bed rest until I'm thirty-two weeks along.

Blake repacks the overnight bag Delanie prepared for me, helps me dress, and a nurse wheels me down the long hall toward the elevators.

As we pass room 407, the soft whimpers of a young girl can't help but capture my attention, and I ask the nurse why she's crying.

"Oh," she whispers, "she lost a baby. Full term. Her first."

Tears well in my eyes, the nurse realizes she's said too much, and she attempts to appease me by patting my arm and remarking the mother is young.

She says, "Many times women go through a devastating loss then have no problems with their next pregnancy."

There won't be a next pregnancy for me.

I place my hand on my stomach and, for a moment, empathize with the childless girl who will eventually be wheeled down this long hall and out to an awaiting vehicle, no baby in her arms. I close my eyes and cry inside.

I will do everything the doctor tells me to keep these three safe.

The following weeks crawl by. Each day I wake, I thank God for another twenty-four hours of development for my children, another day of surviving my bedridden status, another day of Blake loving me.

In the first week, I struggle to accept this unwanted hurdle life has placed in my lane. But by week two, I'm making headway emotionally, realizing each passing hour I keep these three little souls inside me is precious.

From the couch, I do basic accounting work on my laptop, which sits on a tray Blake built me. I attempted working in my lap on day one, but my computer kept sliding down my big belly. My new makeshift desk is comprised of two long legs that sit on the floor and two shorter ones that wedge between couch cushions. Blake sanded and polished my miniature couch table, and when I'm deep into constructing financial spreadsheets, I'm hardly aware it's not my work desk.

When work covets my mind, the fear of losing these babies minifies.

I spend time handing out instructions from the couch, as standing places too much weight on my cervix. I'm allowed up for bathroom visits and showers, the latter of which I savor.

Throughout most of my day, I read or work while shouting orders such as "It's in the third drawer by the refrigerator," "Bottom cabinet in the upstairs bathroom," "At the back-left corner of the garage in a bin." How is it I know where everything is, and I've only lived here three months, yet Blake has been here three years and can barely locate his toothbrush? I guess only mothers keep track of garlic presses, hand soap, doggie shampoo, and scores of other unimportant yet often needed items. Living with Blake reveals he loses just about anything that isn't hung around his neck on a string. He's not as perfect as I once perceived, and, how I love his little flaws.

Blake and I rescheduled our wedding for week thirty-three, Christmas Eve. His idea. The ceremony has suddenly become important to him. I suggested exchanging vows from my bedside would be safer, but he wouldn't hear it. He wants me to be standing in front of him when we recite our vows.

The doctor advised us most triplets are born by thirty-three weeks, but when Blake revealed to her that his favorite day of the year is December 24th, she swooned and said less fanfare until then might be a better idea, anyway. (I swear her crush on Blake deepens every time she sees him.) I'm not sure I'll make it to Christmas Eve without going into labor, but I conceded to his wishes.

He continues to advance in the golf standings. Val has spent lots of nights sleeping upstairs in the bedroom Hux will use on his visits home from college. When Val is pulling a twelve-hour shift, Evy comes. And Jody calls me from Washington every evening, taking my mind off my bedridden status with work and family tales. One or another of my running and high school friends stops nearly every day. Blake has passed out more front door keys than we have houses on our street. When he's not home, friends or neighbors knock and let themselves in.

Since most of these do-gooders are my age, somewhere between raising teenagers and becoming grandparents, they excitedly anticipate rocking babies to sleep. Blake's purchased three of everything: rocking chairs, bassinets, dressers, cribs. The bassinets sit quietly in the nursery that extended our bedroom, and the cribs are perched in the triplets' bedrooms upstairs.

Our newly constructed nursery is white and teal with tall glass windows and lots of light filtering through flowy sheers. Each night before I close my eyes, I stare straight at the bassinets sitting a few feet from me. I smile, then close my eyes, welcoming sleep because I'm sure it will avoid me soon.

All through November, construction workers came and went, mostly ignoring the big blob on the couch and heading straight for our bedroom to knock out walls and design a most glorious nursery. Some steal in the front door and ascend the stairs to add a fourth bedroom to the second floor and convert the third-floor attic into two more bedrooms, both flaunting outlandish outside stairways, which Gianna swears is the most "dope" (I hate that word) house exit ever.

Once when an unsuspecting new, fairly young worker strutted past me, heading toward the nursery, he looked up and came to a dead stop, a horrified look on his face. It appeared his boss forgot to tell him anyone was home.

"Don't mind me," I told him. "I came with the house."

He smiled. I smiled. And for the first time in my life, I am okay with being unnoticed.

Please, God, let these three be born healthy and strong. Let me annoy them for years, and every time they ignore me, I promise to say a prayer of thanks that they are normal children.

Our kids flit in and out with disregard. Sophie and Hannah visit every other weekend, and Delanie drives home nearly every Friday. Hux flies in for Thanksgiving, and we expect him to arrive for his Christmas break a week before the wedding. But no one pays much mind to me these days other than to ask where something is.

Lena and I have become closer in the past two months. She drops off work from Larry, who's learning to manage the office quite well. He and Lena have begun singing at several venues across the city and county. Their popularity boosted his confidence, and as a result, his relationships at work improved. Sherry quips, "he's come out of his cubicle." Even Agnese has warmed up to him.

Miracles. They are all around us.

Lena patiently awaits her stint as the Anderson triplets' nanny. She garnered national press for it, too, insisting the nanny publicity helped her and Larry book more shows around town. Of course, she'll never be a nanny to these three little ones. She'll be their Aunt Lena, a woman whom God placed in our lives (and ours in hers) at exactly the correct moment in time.

Like so many other friendships I have, I'm blessed with hers. I treasure my friends. With the slightest inkling I need help, they pop up around me like sunflowers. My running friends promised to help in the first few months, Jody is flying back to Erie for a week in February, and Val (the nurse) says I couldn't stop her from coming every day after the triplets are born if I hired a platoon of bouncers.

Of course, all of our children—save sweet Hannah—insist they won't change a diaper, but Blake and I know that will change.

After a long and tedious November, December rolls in with new enthusiasm as I head toward couch-prison release day: December 16.

On the morning of the sixteenth, I'm up before sunlight preparing a crockpot of chili and baking cookies for dinner. In the afternoon, I remove my rings and immerse my fingers in hamburger, cheese, onions, and garlic, transforming the beefy concoction into my famous meatballs that I bake, simmer in my mother's best red-sauce recipe, and freeze for Christmas dinner.

Blake scolds me for overworking myself, but I ignore him and spend a wonderful day cooking and meandering around our new home. I haven't been upstairs until now, so I lumber through the colorful rooms with their polished or newly purchased furniture.

Each child selected their wall color, and all five picked different hues. Hux selected a deep purple for the third-story bedroom with the small window, swearing he'll be able to sleep forever in its darkness. Delanie chose a smart, sophisticated cream for a second-floor room, which she spends weekends in, and Gianna selected a loud teal color for the large room on the third floor, which she will share with Sophie when she's in town. The two are closer than twins.

Hannah's selected the smallest room (so like her) on the second floor and painted its walls pastel pink and white. She chose this bedroom because it's the closest one to where the triplets will sleep when they graduate from nursery bassinets to cribs.

We have two rooms reserved for the triplets, one for the boy (Blake is thrilled he's having a boy.) and one for the girls to share. (God help us. Six girls.)

By the end of my first glorious day preparing food and roaming through rooms, I'm still filled with energy, but my back is breaking. I become winded climbing stairs, clearly out of shape from my couch-bound hours.

By the end of my first week up, every muscle and bone of my torso and legs screams at me to lie back down, but I persist, and on December 24th, Blake and I gather in the living room in front of our new fireplace, the preacher, all five kids, Val's family, Evy's family, and Lena and Lawrence.

I've made it to our wedding day.

"Blake, do you take Nikki to be your lawful wedded wife?" the preacher asks, and Blake utters, "I do," with voice cracking and tears falling.

The overhead lights are dimmed, and tiny twinkle lights and candles frame us with a tender glow. *Silent Night* plays softly on an all-Christmas radio channel, and the logs of the fire crackle behind us. Nothing could be more romantic.

"To have and to hold..."

I can't hide my tears. I stare into Blake's eyes and an unfamiliar bliss warms me.

"From this day forward..." A soft, soothing sound envelopes the pastor's words. "For better or for worse, for richer or for poorer, in sickness and in health..."

Yes, I'm thinking, from this day forward we will love each other passionately, fervently, ardently.

"Mom?" Delanie's voice cuts through our vows like a heated knife through an ice cream cake. "Did your water just break?"

It appears the warmth I felt had nothing to do with the ambience.

Chapter Thirty-two - The wedding

An orderly rushes me down a long hall that trails away from the emergency room. I have no underwear on. (I'm pretty sure half of Erie could now identify my vagina in a police sketch.) Blake runs beside us hollering "huff, huff, huff." The kids, all five of them, run behind, arguing with the attending doctor to allow them in the birthing room.

"No," I holler in between contractions. "I don't want anyone in the room but Blake."

We roll past three doorways of fluorescent-lit rooms. Flashes of blue and white scrubs and laborious grunts of women rush by me. Suddenly, some mighty force tips every organ in my body downward as if bone and tissue can't contain them, and this unstoppable urge to push strikes me. Physicality overpowers cognizance and my body, with a mind of its own, pushes without me.

I feel a head crown.

Blake glances down. He must see hair because he has a brief disconnect. He staggers. Hux catches him, Gianna hollers for him to get a hold of himself, and Delanie slaps him across the face.

"Not now," she yells. "You can't do that to my mother!"

He obliges and we hurry onward.

To my amazement when we reach the only vacant delivery room at the end of the hall, there stands the preacher. Blake perks up, setting one hand on my gurney and the other on the wall when the orderly swings me toward the doorway. I jolt to a stop.

"Wait, don't go in there." Blake turns toward Pastor Ryan. "Hurry. I want to be married before they're born."

Doctor Yank and two nurses appear in the doorway. They argue, but Blake doesn't budge.

"Until death do you part." Remarkably, the preacher starts up right where he left off in front of the fireplace at home, his face dismayed.

"I do," Blake shouts.

Pastor Ryan turns toward me. His head snaps back. He cringes as he speaks. "Do you, Nikki, take Blake to be your awful (Freudian), wedded husband…"

"Yes, yes, yes," I shriek.

"For richer or poorer…"

I'm dazed for one-hundredth of a second how this little man has magically appeared and has the gall to ask me questions while I'm crippled in pain. I don't overthink it because a contraction so intense that I can't help but bear down strikes me.

"I do," I scream and grunt at the same time.

Blake yells, "Just marry us."

The preacher, suddenly a terrified look upon him, makes the sign of the cross. I push. A triplet, the boy, slips into Doctor Yank's hands there at the threshold of the delivery room, and the preacher says, "I now pronounce you man and wife."

And that is how one triplet is born out of wedlock, and two, within a loving, healthy marriage.

~~~

Three hours later, I'm reeling in ecstasy and exhaustion as an orderly wheels me into a private room. Although I can't contain the happiness rushing through me, my eyelids droop and my concentration staggers. I doze and wake, waiting for Blake, thanking God for thirty fingers, thirty toes, three sets of formed lungs, strong heartbeats, and vigorous cries. What I had suppressed for months—worry over my age and epilepsy—trickle from me like the last drops of a hard rain. Neither seems to have had ill effects on my children.

I say a *Hail Mary* then an *Our Father*, dozing and thanking, mumbling and napping until the squeak of a door catches my attention.

Evy inches into my hospital room, carrying a bouquet of roses and a slice of wedding cake. "How do you feel?" he asks quietly.

"Not bad." Carefully, I push myself upward in the bed.

He sets his gifts on the hospital stand and, still wearing his garb from the wedding, reaches into his suit coat pocket. "How are the babies?"

"Wonderful. The pediatrician's examining them in the neonatal unit, but their Apgar scores were good. I was able to get two of three to latch onto a breast. Blake will be back to wheel me there for another feeding. I can't walk that far because my episiotomy required so many stitches," I reveal, proudly. Evy hates female deets, and I love ruffling his feathers.

"TMI." He jerks away from me and wrinkles his forehead, squinting as he hands me an unwrapped box that flaunts a local jeweler's logo. "This is for you."

"You bought me something? How sweet."

"Bennet and I have gifts for the babies, but we'll bring those by the house later. This is a little inspiration for strength."

Now, my face wrinkles. "Seriously? I just squeezed three human beings out of my body, if that doesn't prove my strength, nothing does."

He covers his ears with both hands. "If I had known my little visit would develop into an anatomy class, I wouldn't have come."

I chuckle and he drops his arms. "Go on. Open."

I remove the box's lid, lift a shiny gold necklace and dangle it in the air. An odd little engraving with eyes stares back at me. "Evy, you shouldn't have. Is that a stork?"

"No, a peacock."

My stare dances from the charm to Evy. "A peacock? You had a peacock engraved on a charm for me?"

This I know about Evy: he exploits life's intricacies every chance he gets. His visit is about to cascade into an existential lecture. I drop the necklace back into the box and cover my ears.

"Thank you," I say, pressing tight. "I'm sure it symbolizes something I'm lacking."

"Not at all. In eastern Europe, it symbolizes bad luck. That you have an abundance of."

My hands spring to the box, and I thrust it toward him. "Are you crazy? Take this back. I need good luck. You do realize I'll be alone with three babies when Blake is on tour."

"Don't stretch your 'peezy stitches." He waves his hand and takes a seat. "Blake remedied that. He convinced Bennet to sleep in Hux's room when he's out of town."

"And Bennett agreed?"

"Yes, but only because Blake contracted with a twenty-four-hour, on-call nursing company to rescue him if anything runs awry. And he made Val and I agreed to cover for Bennett if he can't make it."

I smile. For as much in the limelight as he is, Blake is truly a man behind the scenes at home. Like a gardener, forever watering my friend-longing petals, his lips eternally curved upwards beneath the shade of his cap.

Evy stands, removes the necklace, and unlatches it. "Lean forward. I'm putting this on you."

"All right." I sigh. "What does it really mean?"

"A peacock symbolizes spiritual awakening, signifies both internal and external growth, rebirth. Many religions believe a peacock's feathers are healing and represent a person's true colors such as integrity, honor, truth, and self-love—all of which you truly do have, Nikki."

"Integrity? Wow."

"Okay, maybe you'll never have that down pat, but the self-love is what I'm getting at." His fingers work the latch, and when it's fastened, he sets a hand on my shoulder, leans, and kisses my cheek. "The peacock means you've learned from your past, have grown, and will use the knowledge you've gained to teach others—your little ones."

I set a hand over my chest then rub the little peacock charm with my fingers. For once, Evy's lecture has coaxed a smile from me. When I gaze upward, I see tears in his eyes.

"I'm proud of you, Nikki." He sniffs, and like a blubbering fool, I lunge forward and encircle his waist with my arms. He leans his cheek on the top of my head. "More and more women are having children later in life after they've found themselves—their feathers flaunting so many colorful eyes. It's brilliant, isn't it? Magnificently brilliant to raise children with so much wisdom."

"I hope you are right, Evy."

"I am." His lips graze the top of my head. "You'll see."

Right at that moment, Blake enters, digests the scene silently for a moment, then rushes forward and wraps his arms around the two of us. Delanie steps in next, then Gianna, and Hux, each of them gingerly shuffling toward us, so that by the time the nurse reenters my room, we are a slobbering scrum of thankfulness.

Epilogue

Three weeks later, when Sawyer, Olivia, and Samantha (Evy insists I've subliminally selected names whose first letters spell SOS.) graduate from the neonatal unit and come home, I stand in the doorway of my bedroom watching our eight children getting to know each other in the attached nursery.

Hannah carefully changes Sawyer's diaper, explaining to Hux, "You have to hold his head until he's a little older." Delanie rocks Olivia in a chair. (I think she's singing to her.) And Sophie and Gianna stand on either side of Sam's bassinet.

"Did she poop, again?" Sophie asks.

Gianna leans her nose in then jumps back like a snapped coil, her nose wrinkled. "Yes, she did." She waves a hand back and forth in front of her face.

"I'll change her." Sophie reaches in.

"No, it's my turn." Gianna nudges her aside.

Right then, my glance catches Delanie, and something beautiful happens. She's gazing at her sister, watching her carefully remove Sam's diaper, when suddenly she turns toward me as if my eyes have burrowed into her heart. She smiles and pantomimes, "I love you, Mom," at the exact moment Gianna glances up.

Gianna's eyes ping from Delanie to me, and she imitates her sister, silent lips forming an "I love you, too." Then I watch and listen. Gently, Gianna replaces Sam's newborn diaper, and softly, Delanie's honeyed humming caresses the room.

Tears fill my eyes. I stand for a long time, enjoying the rare surfacing of my daughters' affection and the selfless warmth all five older kids relay to the three little ones. I love these eight souls more than life itself.

When I finally step out of the room to wipe my eyes and compose myself, I realize Blake is there, staring at me. Just as I have stood loving them, he has stood loving me.

His expression holds an endearment I haven't seen in many years—since my mother first held Delanie in the delivery room on the day she was born.

Her words spring to mind. Words I'd forgotten until right now in this precious moment of time.

A mother's job is to love her children. Yet first, you must learn to love yourself, Nikki. You don't have to be perfect. You just have to be enough. And you will be. Trust me. The simplest of mothers, those who stand in the shadows of their children, are often the strongest souls, their love unbending.

When Hux was born, my mother was there again in the delivery room, supporting me. When they placed Hux in my arms, panic struck me. Frightened that there wasn't enough of me to go around, I cried to my mom, confiding I didn't know how I could raise two little lives. She responded with words that come to mind now.

You raise them with love, Nikki. Love never divides, only multiplies.

Understanding her took many years. I know now that I'm far from perfect—but I am enough. There will be trying times, unfinished jobs, sleepless nights, but in the end, what these children will remember most about me is that I loved them. It's true. Love multiplies. I have plenty to divvy out to these rising eight souls, my dear friends (who move bodies), and I have lots left over for Blake, too.

I gaze deep into his eyes and as I do, he winks and whispers, "You are a great mother, Nikki. I love you."

I slip my hand into his. There is nothing more comforting than a husband who realizes the sacrifices you've made and will continue to make for your children.

"I love you, too," I whisper back, then turn toward our kids. Instantly, he slips his arms around my waist from behind. I lean back on him, smiling. I know we'll have to endure rough patches, yet we'll survive.

Right now, however, I'll enjoy love's sweet serenity.

My heart swells with happiness and as it does, a stunning yet beautiful lightning bolt zigzags across our window and strikes the ground outside, a boom vibrates the house, everyone gasps, the lights flicker then fade, and every appliance from all over our house hisses to a fizzling halt. Blake whispers something to the effect the electrician was right, we need new wiring. Someone cries. I think it's Hannah, but I can't tell for sure because blackness has fallen over every inch of us.

Perfect.

A streak of silvery moon releases from behind a cloud and slithers through the windows, lighting up the silhouettes of my children. Hux passes gas and says, "That scared the crap out of me."

The girls scream at him. The babies compete to win the shrillest newborn wail. Blake chuckles. Furgy barks. And, smiling, I tighten my temporal seatbelt for a long, bumpy ride.

Acknowledgments

Many thanks to my editor, Fiona Branton. You've guided me toward better writing despite my efforts to wander off path. I am convinced you are the best editor in the world, and I am thankful, not only for your unending grammatical skills, but for your patience and honesty. Somewhere over the years of my too-many emails and on-the-fly coffee-date invitations, you have become a trusted friend. Thank you, Fiona. For everything.

I also owe much to the girls who weathered through my unedited version of *Don't Mind Me, I Came with the House*—the pre-Fiona one. First, thank you to Carol Crandall, a much-loved friend, for reading this novel so many times she could recite it. You helped me smooth out the wrinkles and bring home the ending. Thank you, Sharon Desser, Jan Vieyra, Debby Masterson, Laura Lewis, LeAnn Parmenter, and Heather Havern (my wonderful niece). You have eagerly read every in-the-raw novel I've written and helped iron out the kinks. I value your input more than you know. Thank you, too, Beverly BevenFlorez from *Ink and Insights* for the invaluable beta read of that final draft. Your last-minute advice softened the remaining rough patches and helped enhance my storyline.

Thank you to my family, Jeff, Jessie, Zak, and Jilly for loving me despite my habit of infusing your personalities into my characters and plagiarizing your fun-loving pranks. Most of all, thank you to my sweet princess, Layla. Your "Can Gigi talk?" phone calls were a breath of fresh air and just what I needed to break up my long days.

And to my sweet dog, Furgy, whom I try to mention as often as I can. This is the very first novel I've written without you at my feet. I hope you are proud and running free, old girl. Miss you.

About the Author

Cyndie "CJ" Zahner is a digital-book hoarder, lover of can't-put-down books, wife, mother, grandmother, and author.

Before becoming a novelist, CJ worked as a grant and freelance writer. Her articles varied from business to women's health to the paranormal. In 2015, she began looking at life differently when her brother and his wife were diagnosed with dementia and early-onset Alzheimer's. At that time, her husband pulled her aside and said, "Quit your job. You're a writer." After twenty years of service, CJ picked up her purse at work one day and quietly walked away.

Now, she rises before dawn, writes, runs, and smiles much. She's published five novels: *The Suicide Gene* (2018), *Dream Wide Awake* (2018), *Project Dream* (2019), *Friends Who Move Couches* (2020), and *Don't Mind Me, I Came with the House* (2021).

She resides in Wendell, NC and spends summers in the town she grew up in, Erie, Pennsylvania. A hard worker and story lover, Zahner hopes to read, write, and run happily ever after.

If you enjoyed this novel, please consider dropping a review for her on Amazon, BookBub, and Goodreads, or sending her a message at www.cjzahner.com. She promises she reads every comment.

Made in the USA
Coppell, TX
01 March 2023

13622726R10135